She looked

The polite kiss [they had] before should ha[ve ...] might have prob[ably where they] left off.

Fliss moistened her lips with the tip of her tongue, and he found himself watching her almost hungrily. His mouth felt dry. Even now, it was hard to believe she wasn't just a figment of his imagination. For so long, he'd been forced to banish his memories of her to his dreams.

Morgan pulled the chair nearest to her away from the wall and straddled it. He noticed she moved her foot aside to avoid brushing his trouser leg, but although he didn't like it, he pretended not to notice.

"Alone, at last," he said, not without some irony, and then wished he hadn't when she immediately drew back. But he had to go on, and, fixing a smile on his lips, he regarded her encouragingly. "I was beginning to think you were afraid to be alone with me."

Dear Reader,

I was lucky enough to be one of the authors who spearheaded the Harlequin Presents® line in North America, and you can imagine my delight when I was asked to write the story which celebrates not just the 2000th book in Presents™, but also the new millennium.

Writing has always been a source of great satisfaction and enjoyment to me, and it's been a similar thrill to hear that you enjoy my books, too. Believe me, there is no better reward for a writer than to earn the approval of her readers, and your letters make my day.

I expect you've heard that writing is a lonely occupation, but I don't find it so. When I'm writing, my characters keep me company, and I'm so busy trying to sort out their lives that I hardly have time for my own.

I hope you enjoy **Morgan's Child** and can identify with Morgan's and Fliss's problems. When a man returns from the dead, there's no doubt that it must turn everyone's world upside down. Will Fliss marry Graham, the man she's come to rely on, or will the new millennium create a new beginning for her and Morgan? I hope you'll enjoy finding out.

I'd like to wish all my readers, old and new, a very happy and successful start to the new year.

Anne Mather

Anne Mather

Morgan's Child

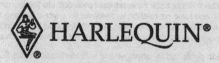

TORONTO • NEW YORK • LONDON
AMSTERDAM • PARIS • SYDNEY • HAMBURG
STOCKHOLM • ATHENS • TOKYO • MILAN • MADRID
PRAGUE • WARSAW • BUDAPEST • AUCKLAND

ISBN 0-373-12000-1

MORGAN'S CHILD

First North American Publication 1998.

Copyright © 1998 by Anne Mather.

This edition published by arrangement with Harlequin Books S.A.

® and TM are trademarks of the publisher. Trademarks indicated with
® are registered in the United States Patent and Trademark Office, the
Canadian Trade Marks Office and in other countries.

Printed in U.S.A.

CHAPTER ONE

FLISS let herself into the cottage and dropped her tote bag onto the iron chest that stood just inside the door. The living room was deliciously warm after the chilly air outside, and after bending to pick up the mail she surveyed her small domain with a certain amount of relief. It had been a long day and she was tired, and it was so nice to think that she had the weekend ahead, two whole days without any demands being made on her.

Well, apart from Graham's coffee morning, she acknowledged ruefully, but that wasn't exactly an arduous affair. She'd promised to make some of her cheese scones, of course, but she could do them in the morning. Scones were always nicest fresh from the oven, and Graham was always so grateful for anything she did for his church.

Dear Graham. She smiled and, crossing the living room, she entered the tiny kitchen that adjoined it. A cup of tea first, she decided, dropping the letters on the counter and plugging in the kettle. Then she was going to take a long hot bath. Graham had his bible class this evening, so she wasn't expecting to see him again until the next morning at the church hall. Which meant she had no one to please but herself.

Not that there was anything the least bit intimidating about seeing Graham, she mused, taking off her cashmere coat and Paisley scarf and hanging them in the understairs cupboard. Indeed, she had a lot to thank Graham for. She couldn't forget all that he had done for her and their relationship had deepened over time. Without him, she might never have found the strength to drag herself out of the hole Morgan's death had thrust her into, and it was in part thanks to him that she now had a home and a job in a place that was as far removed from the ravages of war-torn Nyanda as it was possible to be.

And it was only natural, she thought, that the gratitude she had initially felt towards him should have eventually deepened into a stronger emotion. Graham was that kind of man; all his parishioners loved him, and she was sure Morgan wouldn't resent her finding a less frenetic kind of happiness with another man.

Or would he? As the kettle boiled, she admitted to herself that she didn't really know how Morgan would feel. Their relationship had left little room for that kind of speculation, and there was no doubt that when they had been together no other man had stood a chance.

Her mouth quivered with remembered anguish, and she hurriedly reached for the tea caddy, determined not to let any maudlin thoughts of her dead husband destroy the very real happiness she had found with Graham. Graham wasn't Morgan, and she wouldn't have wanted him to be. Her love for Morgan had been too strong, too passionate, and the pain she had suffered when it had ended so violently had convinced her that perhaps it was better not to feel so deeply. If she'd cared for Morgan as she cared for Graham, she would have been distressed when she had received the news of his death but she wouldn't have been devastated; she wouldn't have felt that life no longer had any meaning; that her whole world had fallen apart...

The sound of the phone broke into her reverie, and she was grateful. From the beginning, the doctor had warned her not to brood about the past, and she was gradually coming to terms with it. Morgan was dead. They'd found the remains of his body in the burnt-out car. That period of her life was over, and she told herself that she had stopped looking back.

Squaring her shoulders, she picked up the phone. 'Hello,' she said cheerfully. 'Whittersley 2492.'

'Felicity?'

Fliss expelled a breath. Of all people, she thought rue-fully, but her mother-in-law called her so infrequently these days that she wasn't altogether sorry. 'Yes, it's me,' she greeted the other woman warmly. 'Hello, Celia. It must have been at New Year that I last spoke to you and James.'

'Yes, well—'

There was a wealth of unspoken censure in those two small words, and Fliss prepared herself for another gentle tirade on what Celia and James Riker thought of their only daughter-in-law's removal to this small Wiltshire village, which was so remote from the life they lived in Sussex. She dreaded to think how they would react when they learned that Graham had actually asked her to marry him.

In all honesty, she hadn't wanted to mention it at New Year anyway, as those particular celebrations always brought back memories of Morgan. They'd always spent New Year together, and an image of them sharing a glass of champagne could still upset her even after all this time.

She sighed, nudging the solitaire diamond ring on her finger with some trepidation. She had to concentrate on Graham, and the life they expected to build together in the coming year. A year which would bring in a new millen-nium; a new husband. Was this a suitable moment to tell the Rikers the truth?

'Um—' Celia seemed to be finding difficulty in going on and, taking the initiative, Fliss swallowed any lingering doubts.

'I was going to ring you anyway,' she said, but before she could get any further Celia found her voice.

'Oh, why?' she asked. 'Have—have they been in touch with you?' The tremor in her voice caused a sympathetic shiver to slide down Fliss's spine. 'The Foreign Office, I mean?'

Fliss swallowed again. 'The Foreign Office?' she echoed, trying to sound casual and failing, abysmally. She sought the safety of the nearby sofa's arm. 'I—why, no.' She moistened suddenly dry lips. 'Have they been in touch with you?'

Her thoughts spiralled. What now? she wondered. She'd thought she was through with all the formalities consequent upon Morgan's death. And it had to be about Morgan. There was no other reason for the Foreign Office to get in touch with her.

The silence at the other end of the line was ominous, and although she quite understood that anything to do with the death of their son was just as painful for her in-laws as it was for her she wished Celia had marshalled her facts before picking up the phone.

'You haven't had a letter, then?' her mother-in-law queried at last, and Fliss knew an uncharacteristic urge to scream that that was what she'd just said. 'About—about the coup in Nyanda,' Celia added confusingly. 'Oh, dear. James said you would have rung us if you had.'

'The coup in Nyanda?' Fliss couldn't imagine why the recent coup in the country where Morgan had met his death should be of any interest to her. Indeed, she preferred not to think about Nyanda at all, and the news that her husband's killers had overthrown the legal government was too painful to think about.

'Yes, the coup,' Celia repeated eagerly, and Fliss wondered if there was to be some kind of official acknowledgement of Morgan's murder. Surely they were not hypocritical enough to suggest that there should be some lasting memorial? The last thing she wanted was to have all those unhappy memories raked up now.

She tamped down her indignation, and said, 'Is there a problem?' in what she hoped was a pleasant tone.

'You could say that.' Celia's response was agitated. 'Oh, Felicity, it's such wonderful news!'

Fliss felt guilty suddenly. Here she was considering only her own feelings when it was obvious that Morgan's mother was delighted by what she'd heard. The trouble was, since she and Graham had started spending so much time together, she'd been neglecting her in-laws. How long had it been since she'd visited them at Tudor Cross?

'Celia—'

She didn't know exactly what she'd been intending to say, but her mother-in-law broke in before she could go on. 'Morgan's alive!' Celia cried, and then collapsed into violent sobbing and Fliss heard Morgan's father swear as he grabbed the phone from her.

The room swam dizzily around her. She was glad she was sitting down, but even so the feeling of imbalance made her feel slightly sick. Clutching the arm of the chair, she assured herself that Celia must be having some kind of seizure. Whatever communication she had had, it could not have said that Morgan was alive.

'Felicity!'

She was dimly aware that James Riker was speaking to her now and his voice, so like his son's, had a sobering effect. She knew he was going to tell her to discount what his wife had said, but Celia's words—so pathetic in some ways, so cruel in others—were not so easily dismissed.

'Felicity,' James said again. And then, more gently, 'Fliss.' He heaved a sigh. 'God, I'm so sorry, my dear. Celia promised me she'd just ask you if you'd had a letter. She wasn't supposed to blurt out what it said.'

'What it said?' Fliss trembled, trying hard to remain calm in the face of enormous provocation. 'I just don't know why you thought I'd be interested in some coup they've had in Nyanda.' She drew a breath. 'Are they planning a memorial to all the innocent victims of the war, or what?'

'Oh, Fliss.'

James sounded so distressed now that Fliss wished she could say something to reassure him. It seemed there had been a letter and somehow Celia had convinced herself that

Morgan was still alive. How awful for her husband to have to deal with that, and handle his own grief as well.

'It's all right,' she said, putting aside her own feelings. 'It's obvious Celia's got the wrong end of the stick. If there's anything I can do, please feel free to call me. Um— perhaps if there is to be a memorial service we could get together—'

'Oh, Fliss!'

Her words didn't seem to have reassured him at all, and she hoped he didn't think she didn't care. No one liked the suggestion that a relative might not be wholly rational, but if he'd had any doubts about Celia's mental capacity he shouldn't have let her make the call in the first place.

'Felicity,' he said again, and she registered the return to a more formal appellation with a relieved smile. 'You did hear what Celia said, didn't you?'

Fliss nodded. Then, realising he couldn't see her, she answered, 'Yes, of course.'

James groaned. 'You heard, Fliss. But you weren't listening,' he interposed swiftly. 'God, I knew we should have driven down to see you instead of expecting you to call us. But the weather's been so abominable, and we've both had flu—'

'Wait!' Now Fliss broke in. Before he said another word, she had to know what he meant. 'Are—are you saying there's some truth in what Celia was saying? Is there some doubt about—about Morgan's death?'

'Not doubt, no.' As Fliss gripped the receiver with hands that were now ice-cold and trembling, her father-in-law gave what sounded like a muffled laugh. 'Oh, my dear. There is no doubt. Morgan *is* alive. He's apparently been a prisoner of the rebel forces for the past four years.'

Fliss couldn't believe it. She had the awful feeling that this was some sort of practical joke. Morgan was dead. The Foreign Office had virtually said so. They'd found the burnt-out remains of the car he'd been travelling in on the airport road, and the chances of Morgan having survived the ambush were minimal.

'You obviously haven't watched the reports on television,' her father-in-law continued, his voice a little unsteady. 'The rebel leader, a man called Julius Mdola, gave an interview outside the parliament buildings in Kantanga, and he admitted he'd been forced to keep his whereabouts a secret because of the danger of attack.' He made a choked sound. 'The authorities believe Morgan must have been with him, and, thank God, they've discovered he's still alive.'

Fliss shook her head as if to clear it. She could hear James's voice, but the things he was saying made no sense. Whatever lies he'd been told, she didn't want to hear them. It was all a mistake, and she just wanted to be left alone.

'Fliss! Fliss, are you still there?' James sounded anxious now, but still she didn't speak. 'Did you hear what I said? They're calling it the coup of the millennium. Mdola insisted it was the people's coup. But as long as Morgan's free I don't particularly care.'

Fliss's mind wouldn't function. Whether she believed it or not, no one could drop a bombshell like that and still expect her to respond. She had to keep telling herself that the Rikers were mistaken. Whatever they said, Morgan wasn't coming back.

'Fliss, for God's sake, answer me!'

James was getting angry now, and Fliss supposed that she couldn't blame him. It wasn't his fault that her mind had slipped out of gear. Well, it was his fault, but there were obviously mitigating circumstances. If Graham were here, he'd know how to deal with it. He always knew what to do in a crisis.

'Fliss, I know you're there,' James declared at last, a trace of desperation in his voice, and she guessed he had detected her quickened breathing. 'You should have had a letter,' he added, somewhat flatly. 'When I rang the Foreign

Office earlier today, they confirmed that you'd been contacted, too.'

Fliss shook her head again, wondering if she was the only sane person amongst them. 'James, it's not true,' she said firmly, trying not to get impatient. 'Whatever you've heard, Morgan is dead.' She licked her lips. 'You saw the pictures of that car, just as I did. No one could have survived—' She broke off. 'And now, if you don't mind, I don't want to talk about it any more.'

'Oh, hell!' James swore. 'Look, my dear, I know this has come as a shock to you, and I'm sorry you've had to hear the news so baldly. But it is true. Morgan's alive. He's presently in a hospital in Kantanga. Some kind of stomach infection, I believe.'

'No—'

'Yes.' James sighed. 'You will forgive Celia, won't you? She was so excited, she couldn't wait to talk to you.'

Fliss couldn't breathe. 'No,' she said again, seemingly incapable of saying anything else, and Morgan's father groaned.

'Yes,' he insisted. 'Look, we'll come down and see you. Not tonight, of course, but we'll be with you first thing in the morning.'

Fliss didn't answer him. There was a buzzing in her head, and although she knew the lamps in the room were lit she could sense a darkness at the corners of her eyes. She slid numbly off the arm of the sofa, bouncing briefly on the chintz-covered cushions before slipping almost nervelessly onto the floor. The phone dropped from her fingers, but she didn't notice. As the blackness engulfed her, she heard Morgan's father saying her name over and over again...

She recovered consciousness to the sound of someone hammering at the door.

For a moment, she didn't know where she was, and even

the realisation that she was lying on the rug in front of the stone hearth didn't immediately supply an explanation. Had she tripped and fallen? Had she hit her head? She couldn't remember ever having fainted, but it seemed obvious that she wouldn't have just lain down in front of an unlit fire.

Her head was throbbing quite badly and whoever was attacking her door wasn't improving it. If only they would stop banging quite so loudly, she might find the where-withal to think.

'Fliss!' The letterbox rattled and someone shouted her name through the opening. 'Fliss, can't you answer me? Where are you? Are you all right?'

It was Graham, she realised as the pause in the knocking allowed her brain to function again. Graham was at her door, and she couldn't understand why he sounded so worried. She distinctly remembered him telling her that he was giving a bible class this evening. He should have been at the vicarage, not hammering on her door.

She shook her head, and then wished she hadn't when the room spun dizzily about her. Obviously, she had fainted, she thought incredulously. But how had Graham known that she needed his help?

She struggled up onto her elbows. She'd always believed she wasn't the type to suffer sudden losses of consciousness. She'd thought she was made of stronger stuff and it was disconcerting to discover she'd been wrong. Why, even when she'd heard the news that Morgan had been murdered by the rebels—

Morgan!

The searing recollection of what she was doing on the floor hit her with lightning force. For a second, she was half afraid she was going to lose consciousness again, but Graham chose that moment to renew his assault on the door. Oh, God, *Morgan,* she thought sickly; Morgan's alive. And, struggling groggily to her feet, she saw the phone receiver dangling from its cord.

'Fliss!' The letterbox rattled again. 'Oh, Fliss, darling, can't you open the door? Can you hear me, Fliss? Oh, dear, I'm going to have to break a window. I've got to see that you're all right.'

Graham!

Rubbing a dazed hand across her damp forehead, Fliss managed to regain her balance. 'I'm—here. I'm all right,' she called in a thin, wavery voice. Replacing the receiver and using the furniture for support, she started across the room. 'Just give me a minute. I can't seem to find the key.'

'It's on the floor,' said Graham, bending to speak through the letterbox again. 'Thank God you're all right. I've been so worried. I managed to push your key out, but you've dropped the dead bolt so I couldn't use my key.'

Fliss allowed her tongue to moisten lips that were as dry as parchment and bent to gather up the key. Of course, she thought, making sense of what he was saying, as this cottage still belonged to the church, it was feasible that Graham should have a key. The fact that she had had dead bolts fitted along with the existing locks had been an added security precaution on her part. She was used to living in London, where excessive personal protection was the norm.

It took a few moments for her trembling fingers to fit the key into its hole and deal with the other locks, but at last she got the door open. And, as if his patience had been stretched to breaking point, the Reverend Graham Bland— her fiancé—burst into the room, grasping her by the shoulders and pulling her into his arms.

'Fliss!'

His voice was thick with emotion, and she wondered why her phone being off the hook should have caused him such concern. How long had she been unconscious, for heaven's sake? He was behaving as if he knew something was wrong.

'Should—shouldn't you be at bible class?' she ventured at last, when he drew back far enough to stare into her pale face. His expression gave her an anxious feeling. Did she look as numb as she felt?

'At bible class?' he said, shaking his head. 'My dear, I came as quickly as I could. When the Rikers phoned me, I was—shattered. Finishing the bible lesson was the least of my concerns.'

'The Rikers phoned you?' Fliss felt a momentary twinge of the dizziness that had overwhelmed her before. 'So—so you know what they—what they were ringing me about?'

'Well, yes.' Graham cupped her face in his large hands now, and smoothed her cold cheeks with tender fingers. 'Oh, my dear, I can imagine what a shock this has been for you. The Rikers were frantic when you went off the phone.'

Fliss nodded, but although she was trying hard to behave rationally she couldn't seem to stop shaking. Hearing that the Rikers had told Graham the same thing they had told her made it more official somehow. Her fears—her doubts that maybe she had been hallucinating—were all swept away by Graham's assertion. He wouldn't have said it if it wasn't so. By some miracle, Morgan was alive. In a few days—weeks?—he'd be coming home.

CHAPTER TWO

HOME...

Fliss shivered, staring up into Graham's kind, familiar features with a growing sense of panic. This wasn't Morgan's home, she realised numbly. It never had been. The home she'd shared with Morgan had had to be sold when she couldn't afford to go on paying the mortgage.

Besides, she remembered dully, she hadn't wanted to go on living in the house she'd shared with her husband when he was alive. There'd been too many ghosts; too many memories. When Aunt Sophie had told her about the teaching job that was going at the village school, she'd practically jumped at the chance to get away from London. Whittersley was her home now. She had eventually succeeded in putting the past to rest.

Because of Graham...

She blinked. 'I don't understand,' she said now, unable to deal with such disturbing details at the moment. 'Why would the Rikers contact you? Why not Aunt Sophie? Or the police?'

Graham sighed, drawing her close again before urging her towards the sofa and ensuring that she sat down before he went on. 'I imagine because you'd told them about us,' he declared reasonably, lowering his bulk beside her. 'And your aunt's away, remember? Which is just as well. They wouldn't have wanted to disturb her with such upsetting news at her age.'

Upsetting!

Fliss looked down at her hands enclosed within one of Graham's hands in her lap and felt a different kind of guilt. She should have told the Rikers about her and Graham getting engaged when she'd had the chance, she acknowledged tensely. But she'd never dreamed that something like this might happen, hadn't imagined there might be a time limit on telling them she'd fallen in love with someone else.

It would have been so much easier now if they had been forewarned of her intentions. Easier for Graham, too, she conceded, guessing he might suspect she had put off telling her in-laws about him because she still had doubts. She didn't honestly know why she had avoided telling them about her engagement. She'd known it would never be easy. The Rikers could never replace their son, whereas she—she could marry again.

And Graham could never take Morgan's place in her affections, she appended swiftly. He wouldn't want to. That kind of love happened only once in a lifetime, and perhaps that was why she'd kept her news to herself. How could she explain what Graham meant to her? It was something she'd known they'd never understand.

She took a deep breath, once again avoiding a difficult situation. 'I can't believe it,' she said. 'They were so certain it was Morgan's remains they'd found. Or at least—' she shuddered '—they believed it was the car Morgan was travelling in. Why did they tell us he was dead if there was any doubt?'

'It was virtually a war zone, Fliss,' Graham reminded her. 'I don't suppose it was possible to make any absolute identification at that time. There were human remains among the ashes, and didn't you tell me they'd found your husband's watch?'

'What was left of it,' murmured Fliss, feeling sick. 'But they should have told us he might still be alive if they weren't sure.'

'But they didn't,' said Graham gently. 'And be thankful that the news is good. Would you rather they were writing to tell you that they'd made a mistake and he was dead? How would that make you feel?'

Fliss blew out a breath. She honestly didn't know how she felt. For so long she'd considered herself a widow. She'd just come to terms with that, and now she was expected to accept that it had all been a terrible mistake. And what had James meant, she wondered, when he'd said Morgan had been living with the rebels for the past four years? Surely there must have been some way he could have contacted her; let her know he was alive and not dead.

'I suppose you're right,' she said now, wishing she didn't feel so confused. She glanced about her somewhat dazedly. 'What time is it? Have I been unconscious long?'

'Not long,' said Graham reassuringly, lifting his hand to touch a tender spot on the side of her head. 'I think you must have knocked yourself out on the corner of the sofa. That was why I had such a hard time bringing you round.'

Fliss caught her breath. 'I suppose I ought to ring Morgan's mother and father; let them know I'm all right.'

'No, I will,' said Graham firmly, squeezing her hands for a moment before releasing her. 'They felt they had to call me because your phone was off the hook.'

'I see.'

Fliss moved her head in a cautious nod, and Graham got to his feet. 'I must say,' he added, 'I'm surprised they sprang the news on you so recklessly. Had you had no warning? Haven't the authorities been in touch with you?'

'Well...' Fliss turned her head towards the small pile of envelopes she could just see residing on the end of the kitchen counter. 'There might be a letter,' she confessed, 'but I haven't looked at the mail. All I usually get are bills, and I'm afraid I thought they could wait.'

'Never mind.' Graham bent to give her a swift hug before moving away. 'So long as you're all right, that's all I care about. Now—I'm going to make you a cup of tea and then I'll make that call.'

Fliss forced herself to relax against the cushions, giving herself up to the comforting protection Graham always of-

fered. What would she do without him? She'd come to
depend on him so much. He was so big and gentle—and
capable. Yes, that was it; she'd always felt so safe in his
arms.

But no longer.

With a start, the remembrance of what the Rikers' phone
call was going to mean caused her to stiffen. Oh, God, she
thought, here they were discussing how she'd heard the
news without really considering the consequences of it.
Morgan was alive. Until that moment, she hadn't really
absorbed the concept of what that really meant in terms of
the future. Her husband wasn't dead. However unbelievable
that sounded, it was true.

She remembered suddenly how angry she'd been when
Morgan had first told her he was going to Nyanda.

'You can't,' she'd declared hotly, when he'd told her
about the call he'd had from Paul Giles. 'For God's sake,
Morgan, there's a war going on in Nyanda, and it's not as
if you work for the company any more.'

'But I did,' he'd reminded her mildly. 'And I'm only
going out there to dismantle a few old missiles. I shan't be
involved in the fighting. According to Paul, the rebels have
all been confined to the northern half of the country.'

'And what if they haven't?' Fliss had protested. 'What
if they attack Kantanga? What if there's a coup?'

Morgan's mouth had tilted in a lazy grin. 'What a lot of
"what ifs", my darling,' he'd teased her lightly. And then
he'd said, gathering her closer, 'Just think of the homecom-
ing we'll have when I get back.'

But he hadn't come back. Not then...

'What is it?'

Graham had come back and was looking at her with anxious eyes. Had he considered what this would do to *their*
relationship? she wondered. He'd given her his love and so
much more. She'd known a feeling of security with him

she'd never known with Morgan. Whatever happened, she didn't want to let him down.

'I—just can't believe this has really happened,' she said, not altogether untruthfully. But how could she tell him of the fears she had now? She looked up at him wistfully, remembering how happy she had been when he'd put his ring on her finger. 'I feel as if it's some weird dream; that any minute I'm going to wake up.'

'But you know it's not a dream,' said Graham gently, taking the hand she held out to him. 'My darling, this is going to take some getting used to for—for all of us.' He bent and kissed her knuckles. 'Morgan's your husband. However much I love you, I mustn't forget that. I have to accept that he has the—prior claim to your affections now.'

'No!' Fliss gazed up at him with troubled eyes. Whatever happened, she thought, she didn't want to lose Graham's love. 'I love you,' she said fiercely. 'I can barely remember Morgan.' She caught her lower lip between her teeth. 'You have to believe me. I couldn't bear it if you deserted me now.'

'Fliss—'

'It's true.' She was adamant, getting up from the sofa to gaze searchingly into his face. 'We'd only been married for a few months when Morgan—when he was reported missing. We hadn't known one another as long as I've known you.'

Graham heaved a sigh. 'Oh, Fliss.' He ran a finger round the inside of his dog collar as if it suddenly felt too tight. 'That's not the point, my dear. You know how much I want us to be together. But we can't ignore the facts, no matter how great the temptation may be.'

Fliss stared at him, pulling the braid in which she always wore her hair for school over one shoulder and combing her fingers through its tuft. 'Oh, Graham,' she said in an anguished voice, 'what am I going to do?'

'You're going to have that cup of tea,' declared Graham

practically, marching back into the kitchen. 'And then I'll speak to your in-laws,' he called over his shoulder. 'It's time we told them that you're all right.'

Fliss could hear the kettle boiling now, and presently she heard the rattle of the teapot lid as Graham poured the water into the pot. His large hands moved so clumsily among the china cups and saucers, and she walked to the doorway to watch him setting two of each on the tray.

Fliss's eyes filled with affection. Although he hadn't spent a lot of time at the cottage, he was quite familiar with domestic tasks. He had a housekeeper at the vicarage, but Mrs Arnold was quite elderly, and he was not averse to helping out on occasion.

But there was no denying that he dwarfed his surroundings. Everything about Graham was large, from his size ten shoes to his six feet something in height. He was too heavy, of course, and Fliss had declared that after they were married he would have to go on a diet. But until then Mrs Arnold's fare of suet pastry and steamed puddings would continue to do his health no good.

'There.'

He picked up the tray and followed her into the living room again, but before he could pour the tea someone knocked at the door. Fliss tensed, but it was only Mrs Arnold, who'd come to find the vicar. Old Mr Crabtree was very poorly, she said, and his son had called to ask if Reverend Bland could come at once.

'Damn!' Graham seldom swore, but he was obviously frustrated at that moment. 'Will you be all right, Fliss?' he asked anxiously, after sending Mrs Arnold on her way. 'I'll try to get back later, but I'm afraid it may be too late to make that call.'

'I'll do it,' Fliss assured him firmly, accompanying him to the door and helping him on with his coat. 'It's probably better if I make it anyway. I don't want them thinking I'm in a state of collapse.'

'Even if you are,' remarked Graham drily, buttoning his overcoat. 'Now, are you sure you'll be all right on your own? I can always ask Mrs Arnold to come back and keep you company.'

'I'm fine,' she insisted, ushering him out of the door and then closing it again with rather more urgency than tact. But the last thing she needed was Mrs Arnold gossiping about what had happened. And, despite what she'd said, she doubted she'd ever feel all right again.

The Rikers arrived the next morning.

Fliss was drinking her umpteenth cup of coffee when she heard the car outside, and she wondered if it was the caffeine that was responsible for the rawness of her nerves. She should be thinking about Morgan, dammit, stuck in some hospital in Kantanga, without anyone he cared about around him. Instead of which, she was feeling sorry for herself. What kind of a wife had she turned out to be?

Graham had rung at half-past seven that morning. He'd apologised for not getting back to her the night before and hoped she'd managed to get some sleep. Fliss assured him she had, though in actual fact she hadn't. She'd gone to bed, but she'd stared at the ceiling for most of the night.

And it had turned out that he was ringing not just to enquire about her health but also to assure her that he didn't expect her to attend the church's coffee morning. It went without saying, he said, that on this occasion they would have to do without her famous scones. It was only as he spoke that Fliss realised how remote from ordinary events the whole situation was. Until then, that element of unreality had prevailed.

The trouble was, deep down, she still harboured some bitterness towards her husband. She didn't resent the fact that he was alive, of course—although even now she still found that hard to accept. What she was bitter about was the fact that Morgan had chosen to put his life in such danger. When she'd believed he was dead, she'd been forced to forgive him. Discovering he was alive reminded her of how reckless he had been.

It wasn't as if he'd had to go to Nyanda. He had been a writer, for God's sake, and he didn't owe his old firm any favours. He'd left the Giles Corporation eighteen months before when he'd sold the manuscript of his first novel. It was based on his experiences in Bosnia, and his agent had been sure it would be an immediate success.

He'd joined the army after leaving university, but when he'd met Fliss he'd wanted to stay in one place. As an electronics expert, his job with one of the largest missile specialists in the country had seemed ideal for the purpose, until he'd seen the after-effects of a missile attack on a Bosnian village and had second thoughts.

The idea to try and put his experiences down on paper had been his salvation, and only the fact that the job in Nyanda entailed decommissioning missiles that General Ungave's men had captured from the rebels had persuaded him to accept Paul Giles's request. The money was good, he'd told Fliss, and the experience wouldn't be wasted. At least there would be fewer missiles for the rebels to use.

So he'd gone, and look what had happened. Despite all his promises, he'd disappeared and they'd been told he was dead. And now he was back—well, almost—and she was supposed to welcome him with open arms. Where had he been? What had he been doing? Why hadn't he let them know he was still alive?

But thoughts like these were far too upsetting, and she had to maintain an optimistic front for the Rikers' sake. Besides, she was glad he was alive; she was just confused, that was all, she told herself. It was bound to take some time to sink in.

'Oh, Fliss!'

As expected, Celia burst into tears as soon as her daughter-in-law opened the door. Fliss barely had time to invite

them in before Morgan's mother had gathered her into her
arms, and she found her own face was wet when she let
her go.

'I'll put the kettle on,' she said, glad to escape her father-
in-law's searching gaze. Last night she'd found it hard to
offer anything positive, and it was obvious that Morgan's
parents expected her to share their joy.

Celia followed her into the kitchen, and stood pressing
her hands down onto the cool surface of the counter. A
small woman, with greying blonde hair and blue eyes, she
was obviously in a state of barely suppressed agitation, and
Fliss hoped she wasn't going to let them down.

'It's such wonderful news!' Celia exclaimed, not for the
first time, and Fliss managed a matching smile. 'To think,
just a couple of days ago James and I were discussing the
fact that it was almost four years since—since Morgan disappeared.' She caught her breath. 'Oh, Felicity, I can't believe he's coming home!'

'When—when is he coming home?'

Fliss knew her words lacked the same enthusiasm, but
Morgan's mother didn't seem to notice. 'Well—according
to the letter—you did read the letter, didn't you? You said
last night you'd found it among your other mail.' Fliss nodded, and she continued, 'They say he's suffering from some
kind of stomach infection. Is that a polite way of saying
he's had dysentery, do you think?'

'I—I don't know—'

Fliss hadn't thought of that, and she was grateful when
Morgan's father intervened. 'It could be something minor,'
he said, 'or it could be some tropical infection. Let's not
go jumping to conclusions before we know.'

'Anyway,' went on Celia, 'James spoke to the Foreign
Office again this morning. He wanted to find out if we
could fly out to Nyanda ourselves.' She grimaced. 'But with
all the inoculations we'd need, and the fact that there are

still patches of resistance in the country, we've been advised to wait until he can come home.'

Until he came home...

Fliss's hand shook as she made the tea, but no one seemed to think there was anything unusual in that. They'd all had a shock. Dear God, that hardly covered the way she felt. She was shaking in her shoes at what it meant.

'Thank goodness that dreadful General Ungave has been overthrown,' Morgan's mother remarked now, and Fliss had to bite her tongue at the memory of her in-laws practically rebuking her for not wanting Morgan to go. Morgan's father had been in the military too, before he'd retired to Sussex, and it was because of him that Morgan had joined the army himself. 'I believe the new president, General Mdola, went to school in England. He's quite an educated man, I believe.'

Fliss nodded, concentrating on pouring milk into the jug to add to the tray, and Morgan's father took up the strain. 'I wonder if the fact that we're just a few months from the millennium is significant?' he said. 'I know they're calling it the Millennium Coup, but the rebels had been fighting for quite a long time.'

Fliss looked up. 'What do you mean?'

'Well...' James Riker looked thoughtful. 'It's possible they've had some help from the West. The oil reserves in Nyanda are quite considerable, you know. And Ungave was beginning to get a little greedy, I think.'

Fliss stared at him. 'You mean—this could have happened sooner? The West could have helped the rebels all along?'

'Well, perhaps.' He looked a little uncomfortable now. 'But so long as Ungave didn't—didn't—'

'Make any waves!' Fliss caught her breath disbelievingly. 'The Millennium Coup! What a joke!'

'Felicity—'

'Oh, it doesn't matter.' Fliss picked up the tray now, and

carried it into the other room. She schooled her features. 'Come and have some tea. I believe I've got some biscuits in the cupboard.'

'Felicity.' Obviously Morgan's father wasn't happy with her reaction, and she stood silently while he commanded his thoughts. 'No one knew that Morgan was alive, or—or of course the government would have made representations to get him out. We must view what has happened as—as a bonus. Now, sit down, my dear. You still look very shaken to me.'

'We all are,' said his wife, using a tissue to blow her nose, and then, sitting down on the sofa, she patted the seat beside her. 'Come and sit down, Felicity. We've got wonderful plans to make. You must both have a proper holiday when Morgan gets back.'

A holiday!

Fliss hung back, hoping Morgan's father would take the seat beside his wife, but he didn't and she was obliged to do so. The trouble was, she didn't seem able to share their excitement, and she thought what a selfish cow she was. It should have been the happiest day of her life, but it had been too long in coming.

'Anyway, thank goodness we were able to reach Reverend Bland last evening,' said James into the vacuum, seating himself in the armchair opposite. He smiled at Fliss. 'I remembered you'd mentioned his name, saying what a good friend he was. I felt sure he was the ideal person to help you. With your aunt being away I assumed you wouldn't mind.'

'Oh—no.'

Fliss swallowed, realising there was no way she could reveal how close a friend Graham had become. She glanced down at her hands, wondering if they had noticed she wasn't wearing her wedding ring on the right finger. Would she ever wear Graham's engagement ring again?

Thankfully, the Rikers kept the conversation going while

they drank the tea and ate several of the chocolate biscuits Fliss had found. Celia confessed she'd not been able to eat any breakfast, though she wouldn't let Fliss make her anything else, and they chattered on about what they were going to do when their son came home.

It was so easy for them, thought Fliss half enviously. But did they really expect her and Morgan to take up where they'd left off almost four years ago? If she'd known he was alive, she could have looked forward to this day. As it was, she felt as if Morgan was part of her past.

'So—' Celia patted Fliss's hand. 'What was it you were going to ring us about? With all the excitement, it went completely out of my head.'

Fliss blanked. 'I beg your—?'

'Last night,' her mother-in-law prompted. 'When you first answered the phone, you said you'd been going to ring us. I just wondered what it was you were going to ring us about. Did you give any thought to spending Easter at Tudor Cross?'

'Oh—' Fliss's mouth dried. She'd forgotten all about the invitation Celia had issued at New Year. It was just after Graham had popped the question, and Fliss had been too anxious about their reaction to give an answer then. 'I—' A lie seemed the only alternative now. 'I can't remember, I'm afraid.'

'Oh, well, never mind.' Celia had too much else on her mind to worry about what her daughter-in-law had been ringing about. 'And in the circumstances no doubt we'll be having a celebration when Morgan comes home. You must come and stay with us when he gets back.'

'Well—'

Once again, Fliss was nonplussed. She felt as if events were moving far too fast for her to handle. They hadn't even heard from Morgan yet, and already Celia was wanting to organise their lives. How could she make any plans? She didn't know how she'd feel when she saw him again.

'Give them time, Cee.' To her relief, Morgan's father chose to intervene. 'We've all had a shock, and I think Felicity needs some breathing space. I know you mean well, but you're rushing things. We don't even know how fit Morgan's going to be when he gets home.'

CHAPTER THREE

MORGAN stood at the window of the quarters that had been provided for him at RAF Craythorpe, watching the rain streaming down the panes. It didn't seem to have stopped raining since he'd stepped off the plane from Lagos the day before, and although he'd dreamed about the kind of gentle rain they got in England the reality was no longer so appealing.

How long were they going to keep him here?

Suppressing his panic, he acknowledged that he was only fooling himself by pretending the weather was responsible for the way he was feeling. He was just using it as an excuse to bolster his confidence. Blaming the rain for the fears and apprehensions that wouldn't go away.

Lifting one balled fist, he pressed it hard against the glass, trying not to give in to the urge to smash his fist right through the pane. He would have liked that, he thought; liked to have shattered the glass and felt the sharp pain of the broken shards digging into his flesh. God knew, he badly wanted to smash something, and only the certain knowledge that his doctors—keepers—would put it down to his uncertain mental state kept him from creating an ugly scene.

But, dammit, they couldn't keep him here indefinitely. All right, he'd been suffering from malnutrition when they released him, but there was nothing wrong with his mind, no matter what they thought. He needed familiar things; familiar people. He just wished he didn't have the feeling that they didn't exist any more.

He took a steadying breath.

The trouble was that although he knew he was free he

didn't feel free. In fact, what he really felt was a shattering sense of disorientation. He'd anticipated that his wife and family would have assumed he was dead, but he hadn't realised how that might affect him now. For so long he'd been forced to blank his mind of any thoughts of loved ones or face the purest kind of mental torture there was.

He sighed. It was hard to remember how he'd felt that morning when his car had been ambushed on the way to the airport. Then, he'd been planning what he was going to do when he got home; looking forward to seeing his wife. He'd missed her so much, and since their marriage they'd spent so little time together. He couldn't wait to get back and tell her how he felt.

The men who'd shot out the tyres of the car and then shot its driver had seemed totally ruthless. It was only later that he'd discovered that because the man had worked for Ungave he was considered expendable. Besides, Mdola didn't take any prisoners. He had no pity for any of Ungave's men who were of no use to him.

Morgan supposed his strongest emotion at that time had been terror, but the fact that he'd survived the attack had sustained him throughout the long trek through the jungle that had followed. It wasn't until they'd reached the rebels' stronghold, in the mountains that bisected the northern half of the country, that he'd had to quell a sense of panic. He might be alive, but he was helpless. So long as General Ungave was in power, they'd never let him go.

The ironic thing was, Mdola had wanted him for much the same reasons as Ungave. He needed Morgan's knowledge of sophisticated tactical weapons to enable him to use the armaments he had. God knew who'd supplied them, but Mdola's men had been equipped with every kind of gun imaginable; mortars; ground-to-air missiles; the list was endless. An arsenal they barely understood.

But the most remarkable thing of all had been that he had recognised Julius Mdola. They'd been at Oxford together, and although they hadn't been close friends at that time they had shared an interest in martial arts. Morgan had been staggered to learn that the man General Ungave had overthrown had been Mdola's uncle, and despite the desperation he was feeling it had been some relief to be able to speak to the man in charge.

His lips twisted. Not that, in the long run, it had done him a lot of good. Despite the fact that Mdola was educated in the West, and could sympathise with Morgan's position, the demands of the situation meant that Morgan had to be treated like any other prisoner. He wasn't imprisoned, of course, in the truest sense of the word, but he wasn't supposed to leave the compound. The only time he had, he'd regretted it. And if it hadn't been for Julius Mdola he knew he'd have been shot.

But would he have survived his captivity if he hadn't become Mdola's friend? he wondered. It was a question he'd had plenty of time to ponder in the years that followed. Would he have kept his sanity if Mdola hadn't allowed him to use the old typewriter they'd kept to churn out their propaganda? Would it have been better if he hadn't survived at all?

He scowled.

He couldn't answer any of these questions. His release had not been the cause for celebration he'd imagined it would be. Would he ever be able to absorb his changing circumstances? Would he ever come to terms with the fact that life had moved on?

But it wasn't just his changing circumstances that was giving him such a sense of anticlimax now. It was more than that; he had the uneasy suspicion that no one wanted him here. Was he a welcome face or just an embarrassment? Would it have been easier for everyone—his wife particularly—if he had been as dead as they'd believed?

Dead!

For the past four years, everyone had thought he'd died

in the inferno they'd made of his car. They'd mourned him; they'd even held a memorial service for him, according to his mother, and a stone had been erected in the churchyard at Tudor Cross.

His scowl deepened. Had she thought he'd be pleased to hear that? he wondered. Had she no conception of how it made him feel? He wasn't dead; he was alive; he didn't want to hear about his funeral service. But most of all he didn't want to feel like an outsider, especially with his wife.

His wife!

His lips twisted. He wasn't sure he knew his wife any more. The alien confrontation they'd had the previous afternoon had left him feeling more confused than ever. He'd expected their meeting to be strained, yes, but not that she'd act like a stranger. And a stranger, moreover, who didn't like him very much either.

He swore, finding a certain satisfaction in hearing the oath leave his tongue. God, he'd never thought it would be easy, but he'd had no conception of just how hard it had proved to be.

Of course, his parents had been present at the time, and it was possible she'd been inhibited by their demands. His mother, particularly, had asked a lot of questions, and Fliss had behaved as if only the older woman had had that right.

His appearance couldn't have helped, he acknowledged. His shaved head—to remove any infestation of lice—and several days' growth of beard on his chin must have looked strange. He looked like a savage, and even though he'd shaved his beard since it wasn't much of an improvement. His hand had been shaking so much when he used the razor that his chin was now covered in cuts.

He supposed he was thinner, too, though that was less of a problem. He'd soon put on weight once he started eating normally again. And his muscles were hard from the physical regime he'd set himself. Apart from its obvious advantages, keeping fit had been another way of keeping sane.

But, dammit, he hadn't been prepared for civilisation. Four years of living with a rebel army had taken their toll. Someone should have warned his wife that he wasn't the man he used to be. He'd seen too many horrific sights, too much killing, to ever view his own life in quite the same way again.

He hunched his shoulders. They'd warned him, of course. Mdola, at first, and afterwards the British authorities in Lagos: they'd all tried to tell him that returning home after so long an absence was bound to cause problems he couldn't foresee. It was going to take time to adapt, for him and for his family. That was why they'd brought him here to the air base at Craythorpe, for expert counselling. They wanted to assess his state of mind; make sure he was fit to live with normal people again.

He snorted. Mdola wouldn't like that, he reflected. So far as he was concerned, it was the West who had been crazy for supporting Ungave's regime. President Mdola now, Morgan thought, still finding the concept incredible. But he was happy for his friend, and proud of the victory he'd achieved.

Even if it had screwed up his own life, he conceded. But then, he hadn't known what was facing him when he'd left England. *A normal life*, he mused. What the hell was normal? If Fliss's reaction was anything to go by, he wasn't sure he wanted to know.

And it was the knowledge that there had been no real communication between him and his wife that was causing him so much soul-searching now. The truth was, he supposed, that Fliss's attitude had struck at the core of his manhood. Her apathy had made him doubt whether he was still a man.

As if he didn't have enough doubts of his own.

It was stupid, he knew, to allow her behaviour to affect

him. Fliss was still in a state of shock; he'd seen that right away. It was ironic, really, because he'd had doubts about his own feelings. He'd even convinced himself at times that he didn't have feelings any more.

Now, all he could think of was, what had she been doing while she'd thought he was dead? It occurred to him that she might even have got married again. God, was that why she'd been so reticent the day before? Because she didn't know how to tell him the truth?

He realised now that secretly he'd always believed she'd be there waiting for him. That he'd harboured the thought that what they'd had had been so special, she'd never seek consolation in the arms of another man. But the woman he'd met the previous afternoon had behaved as if they were merely distant acquaintances. Had she been wearing his ring? He couldn't even remember if she had.

A group of servicemen crossed the parade ground outside at that moment, and Morgan drew back into the shadows of the room, loath to be observed gazing out. The men glanced his way and he guessed his arrival had caused quite an upheaval. The base wasn't large and it wasn't every day they entertained a psycho like him.

He raked unsteady hands over his scalp, feeling the strange prickle of stubble beneath his palms. Once his hair grew back, he'd look less like a gorilla. He might even feel less like one, too, he thought, expelling a weary breath.

Apparently, there was a band of cameramen and media people camped outside the gates of the air base. He wondered if his mother had told him that to compensate for what she'd said about his memorial stone. In any event, all it had done was make him feel even more of a misfit. He didn't like the thought that they were waiting, like jackals, to attack.

He turned back into the room, surveying its bright interior without enthusiasm. The room was comfortable and warm, but impersonal. It was part of the medical facility here at the base and although it was furnished as a sitting room it was just another hospital room.

There was only one familiar item in the room and that was the picture his mother had brought of his and Fliss's wedding. It showed himself and his wife and his parents, a group photograph taken outside the small church at Tudor Cross. He and Fliss had been married from his parents' home because Fliss's parents couldn't be present. Her father had been killed when she was still at college, and her mother had married again soon afterwards and gone to live in the United States.

They'd been so happy on that day, he thought painfully. They'd been living together for over a year, but they'd both wanted to make that commitment, and they'd been sure their marriage would last. Of course, she hadn't wanted him to go away, but that had been their only real quarrel. He'd had every intention of making it up to her when he got back.

When he got back...

The thought stuck unpleasantly in his throat, and, putting it aside, he concentrated on his parents' images instead. They had aged in the last four years, he conceded. His father was quite grey now, yet when this photograph was taken his hair had been a lighter shade of ash than his son's.

Though God knew what colour his hair would be when it grew back, Morgan reflected impatiently. The way he was feeling now, it should be white. Only Fliss didn't look any different from what he remembered. She'd let her hair grow, of course, but apart from that she didn't seem to have changed.

She was so beautiful; so God-damned beautiful, and he knew an uncharacteristic desire to tear the photograph in half. In God's name, he thought bitterly, what was going to become of them? Had she really only been tense, or was she actually living with another man?

His mouth tightened. Dammit, he had to stop torturing

himself like this. He had to concentrate on getting well. The dysentery he'd been suffering from had gone, but the doctors here had warned him it would take time before he could cope with the ordinary demands of living. Even being in crowds disturbed him, and the occasional spells of panic that had punctuated his period of confinement were not likely to disappear overnight.

He flung himself onto the worn hide sofa and reached for the remote-control pad. Surfing through the television's channels, he felt his thoughts drifting away again. He had found it almost impossible to concentrate on anything since he got back, the pages of the journal that had been his lifeline still lying untouched in his bag.

They'd given him a watch and he glanced at it now, wondering how long it had been since lunch. He'd been told to rest before his next session with the therapist, but despite the pills they'd given him he found it hard to sleep.

The strap of the watch felt unfamiliar on his wrist, but he didn't take it off. His mother had said they'd found the remains of the Cartier watch they'd given him for his thirtieth birthday in the burnt-out shell of the automobile. It was that as much as anything that had persuaded Ungave's men that he was dead.

He shuddered, and the taste of the chicken soup they'd served him at lunch suddenly burned the back of his throat. Nausea, like a chilling wave, swept over him, leaving his skin clammy and his forehead moist with sweat. It was images like that that the doctors were trying to get him to talk about. He'd been suppressing the memories for so long, but they were still as sharp as ever.

He was thrusting himself up from the sofa again in an effort to dispel the sickness he was feeling when the door opened behind him. Swiping a hand across his damp forehead, he turned reluctantly to see who it was. Templar, he guessed; Sean Templar. He might have the same initials as the Leslie Charteris character, but Sean Templar was no saint.

But it wasn't Sean Templar. To his amazement—and apprehension, he admitted tensely—it was his wife who stood uncertainly in the open doorway. Dammit, he thought, he'd assumed she'd gone home. The impression the psychologist had given him was that both his wife and his parents had left the base.

'Hi,' she said, hanging onto the handle of the door as if she was afraid that if she let go of it he'd jump on her. Morgan's lips twisted. If she only knew. Far from being horny, he was very much afraid he might be impotent. 'How—how are you?'

The words were clipped and unfamiliar to him. Oh, God, he thought, when would he get used to these polite exchanges again? For the past four years nobody had cared how he was feeling. He'd been expected to obey orders however friendly Mdola might have been.

Fliss hesitated a moment and then, as if realising she couldn't hover in the doorway indefinitely, stepped cautiously into the room. 'Did you sleep well?' she asked, starting as the automatic hinge closed the door behind her, and Morgan had to stifle the desire to ask her why she was here.

'I slept,' he said instead, not prepared to go into the reasons why his sleeping habits were not a subject for discussion. The concept of relaxing when the next breath he took might be his last was so alien to him that he'd forgotten how to sleep soundly any more.

'Good.'

She seemed to accept his answer at face value, her eyes skittering over his guarded face before darting about the room. She was nervous; that was obvious; but he should be grateful that she'd come. After the day before he hadn't thought she would.

'Did you?' he countered, and there was a trace of anxiety

in the gaze that sought his face. 'Sleep well,' he prompted drily, wishing he knew what she was thinking. If she was concerned about him, why was she looking so blank now?

'Oh—' Comprehension dawned and with it a tight smile that thinned her lips. 'Well, yes. Your parents and I were accommodated in the visitors' quarters. It was easier not to leave the base because of the—well, because of the press outside. We're going home later today.'

Alone?

The thought refused to be dislodged, but Morgan determinedly put it to the back of his mind. 'Ah,' he said, trying not to feel aggrieved that he'd been kept in ignorance of their presence. He blew out a breath. 'Why don't you sit down?'

He indicated the sofa where he'd been sitting but Fliss chose one of the straight-backed chairs nearer the door. 'This is fine,' she said, crossing her legs, and his nerves tightened unfamiliarly at the sight of her slim calves.

The idea that she wanted to stay as far away from him as possible reared its ugly head, but he firmly squashed it down again. If he started thinking like that he'd soon be paranoid. The polite kiss she'd offered him the day before should have warned him that they might have problems taking up where they left off. It wouldn't do to upset her. He just wanted to get out of here as soon as he possibly could.

She moistened her lips with the tip of her tongue, and Morgan found himself watching her almost hungrily. Not because she was his wife, he assured himself, but simply because she was a woman. There were a few females he'd come into contact with during his captivity but sex for sex's sake did not attract him.

His mouth felt dry. Even now, it was hard to believe she wasn't just a figment of his imagination. For so long, he'd been forced to banish his memories of her to his dreams.

But she was here now; she was real; and the knowledge was like a surge of pure adrenaline in his veins.

She looked so good. The long black skirt covered her knees, unfortunately, but the neat little vest she wore with it accentuated the narrowness of her waist and the fullness of her breasts. A scarlet shirt and black slouch boots completed her ensemble, the collar of her shirt a perfect foil for her dark hair...

Aware that he'd been staring and that Fliss was waiting rather apprehensively for him to say something else, Morgan pulled the chair nearest to her away from the wall and straddled it. He noticed she moved her foot aside to avoid brushing his trouser leg, but although he didn't like it he pretended not to notice and, folding his arms over the back of the chair, he regarded her without hostility.

'Alone, at last,' he said, not without some irony, and then wished he hadn't when she immediately drew back. But he had to go on, and, fixing a smile on his lips, he regarded her encouragingly. 'I was beginning to think you were afraid to be alone with me.'

'No—' She seemed to make the denial involuntarily, and then hurriedly tried to repair the damage. 'That is—your parents thought it would be easier—*for you*—' she made the insertion hastily '—that way.'

'Did they?' Morgan's mouth twisted. 'I assume you mean my mother. She seemed to do most of the talking, as I recall.'

'She was—excited,' said Fliss awkwardly. 'It's not every day a son returns from the dead.'

'Or a husband,' murmured Morgan wryly, and she offered a rueful smile.

'You've shaved,' she said, as if she'd just noticed, and Morgan wondered what was going on behind that smooth pale mask. Was she pleased to see him? How was he supposed to know? As yet, she hadn't said anything to give him a clue.

Rubbing a hand over his jawline, he decided to take the initiative, and instead of answering her he said softly, 'It wasn't my fault.' She looked startled then, and he continued, 'The ambush, I mean. There was no way I could let you know I was alive.'

Her eyes sought his then, and as if his words had offended her now she gave him a disbelieving stare. 'No way?' she said, through tight lips. 'Yes, the authorities told your father that. They also said you'd known President Mdola. That you'd been working with him for the past four years.'

Morgan sighed. 'Not with, *for*.'

'Is there a difference?'

'I think so.' He drew a breath. 'And it wasn't quite as cosy as it sounds. He needed the knowledge I had of tactical weapons, just as Ungave did, only in a different way—'

'Yes, you helped him to murder innocent women and children,' cried Fliss fiercely. 'And after all you'd said about saving lives!'

Morgan blew out a breath. 'I was a prisoner, Fliss. Whatever you may have heard, whatever lies you may have been told, I was a prisoner, just like anyone else. Maybe knowing Julius saved my life. I suppose I'll never know. But once I'd seen where their headquarters was, once I'd examined their weapons, there was no way they could let me go.'

Fliss quivered. 'If you say so.'

'I do say so.'

'And you couldn't even use the phone?'

'The phone?' Morgan snorted. 'What phone? There aren't any phones in the jungle. And they had more sense than to let me near their radio transmitter. Get real, Fliss. I'm sorry, but there was nothing I could do.'

Fliss smoothed her hands over her knees. 'Well, anyway, you're back now.'

'Yes.' Morgan noticed she didn't say 'home'.

'I expect it all seems very strange.' She chewed on her lower lip. 'Four years is a long time.'

'Yeah.'

Morgan could feel the tension building inside him, and he tried to tamp down his irritation. She was behaving as if he'd been on some kind of pleasure trip. Hadn't she any idea of how desperate he had felt?

'Look,' he said, after the silence had stretched into an ominous chasm between them, 'I know it hasn't been easy for you—' Or for me either, he wanted to add, but he bit back the words. 'And I don't want you to be afraid that I might—well, come on too strong.' He doubted if he could anyway. 'I realise it's going to take a while for us to— adjust to what's happened. But, if we take it slow and easy—' he forced a smile '—who knows? I suppose time alone will tell.'

She nodded, and the chunky braid fell forward over her shoulder. The ebony strands caught the light, exposing glimpses of red and gold, like a fire in the darkness. He remembered when he'd first got to know her he'd thought she was like her hair: soft and silky on the outside, but with an inner heat that exploded his senses and fired his blood.

He closed his eyes abruptly, disturbed by the unexpectedly carnal nature of his thoughts. It was so long since he'd touched a woman, and he couldn't deny he wanted to touch her now. He'd thought his sexual feelings were dormant, but he had only to be alone with her for all the fantasies he'd had about her to come flooding back into his mind. He didn't know what that said about his mental condition, but it made a mockery of his determination to take it slow.

'Are you all right?'

Fliss had noticed the effort he'd had to make to control his emotions, and once again he resented her cool response. Didn't she have any idea of how he was feeling? Didn't she comprehend that he needed understanding, not confrontation?

What if Mdola hadn't overthrown Ungave...?

But that way lay danger. The doctors here had warned him not to dwell on what might have been. He was free; he was back in England; and he had to stop thinking about the past. The fact that his life had hung by a thread for so long had little bearing on his future.

'I'm fine,' he lied now, feeling the pain as his nails dug into the wood. He thrust back his anger, and tried to concentrate on positive images, but her detachment was bloody hard to take.

'Good.'

She was pleating her skirt now, revealing an unexpected nervousness in the way she folded the cloth. But although it should have reassured him it didn't. Why the hell didn't she open up to him?

'Did you miss me?'

He hadn't meant to say that, but it was out now, and Fliss gave him a guarded look. 'Of course,' she said, but somehow he couldn't believe she meant it. If she had, wouldn't she look at him with something more than suspicion in her eyes?

She shouldn't have come back, he thought bitterly. She should have waited until they'd both had time to come to terms with the situation. He had the feeling she thought she was the only one who had suffered during his absence. For pity's sake, it hadn't been an easy ride for him.

She pulled her lower lip between her teeth now, and once again a host of erotic images filled his head. But it was obvious she had no such weaknesses, and when she spoke he had to think hard before his mind was able to shift into another gear.

'I couldn't believe it, you know.'

Morgan concentrated on his breathing. 'No?'

'No.' She seemed to have found a topic she could discuss, and there was even some animation in her face as she went on, 'The letter they sent—well, it didn't seem real somehow. Even after I'd read it, I still couldn't believe you were coming back.'

Morgan could feel his nerves stretching, expanding, unravelling like a ball of string that was strung so thinly he was half afraid it might break. 'I understood my mother told you,' he said tersely. 'Are you saying you had a letter after all?'

'Well, of course I got a letter!' she exclaimed, and he wondered if she realised how stressed he was.

'But you didn't read it?' he asked harshly, feeling his temper rising. 'For God's sake, Fliss, don't you bother to read your mail?'

'Of course I do.' She was defensive now. 'But—but that particular night I was tired, so I put it down in the kitchen and forgot about it.'

Morgan couldn't hide his anger. 'You forgot about a letter from the Foreign Office!' He uttered an oath. 'My God, what could be more important than that?'

Fliss caught her breath. 'I didn't know there was a letter from the Foreign Office,' she protested. 'As I say, I was tired. And all I usually get are bills, anyway.'

Morgan breathed deeply. 'All right. So when you eventually read the letter you didn't believe it.'

'I didn't believe you could be alive,' she amended breathily. 'For heaven's sake, Morgan, we'd been told you were dead. You must appreciate how it was for me.'

'No.' Morgan refused to make it easy for her. 'Tell me,' he invited grimly. 'I'm getting the feeling you weren't best pleased to get the news.'

'That's not true!'

'Then what is true?' he demanded. 'Go on: enlighten me. Tell me how ecstatic it made you feel.'

'It wasn't like that—'

'No sweat.'

'It wasn't.' She swallowed, her hand seeking the gold chain she wore about her throat. 'We—I—was stunned.

Your mother told you, we'd even held a memorial service for you—'

'I know that.' He scowled.

'Then you should understand how—how distressing it was to hear the news.'

Distressing!

Morgan wanted to beat his head against the wall. For God's sake, was she deliberately trying to destroy him? She was using words to describe his return that might more accurately be used to describe his death.

'I think you'd better go,' he said, keeping his tone flat. If he allowed his real feelings to show, she'd run from here to next week. Pressing his hands down on the back of the chair, he pushed himself to his feet. 'Templar—the psycho—will be coming soon, and he doesn't like an audience.'

'Oh, but—' Suddenly, she was reluctant to leave. 'The doctor said you might like to—to talk.'

'We've talked,' said Morgan tightly, swinging his leg across the chair, but he misjudged its height and the heavy article went over. It cracked like a bullet as it landed on the floor.

Fliss jumped to her feet then and, almost simultaneously, the door opened and Sean Templar burst into the room. It made Morgan wonder if the psychologist had been standing with his ear glued to the panels all the time they were talking, ready to intervene if anything untoward occurred.

For a moment, they were all frozen in a ridiculous tableau, and then Templar bent to pick up the chair. 'Is everything all right?' he asked pleasantly, and Morgan heard Fliss muffle a sob.

'What could be wrong?' he demanded harshly. 'My wife was just leaving, that's all.'

And Fliss pressed a hand to her mouth as if he'd struck her, before rushing tearfully out of the room.

CHAPTER FOUR

'So ARE you going to tell me what happened?'

Graham was trying to be patient, but it was obviously difficult for him. In the week since Fliss had returned from Craythorpe, they had had no chance to discuss the repercussions of what had happened, and she suspected he was only here now because she'd practically begged him to come.

Graham was so conscious of his position as the vicar of St Margaret's, and he had no desire to set tongues wagging any more than they already were. But Fliss needed his support; she needed his guidance; and if she didn't talk about what had happened soon she thought she'd go mad.

'It's not easy,' she said now, and Graham gave her a troubled look. 'I don't know what I'm going to do,' she added softly. 'What do people do in circumstances like this?'

'If you don't want to talk about it, then I shan't press you,' Graham ventured quietly, but she wasn't sure whether that was for her benefit or his. It was apparent that he considered this conversation premature. He'd said as much when she'd told him she'd like to keep his ring.

'I want to tell you,' she said now, fidgeting with the glass beside her plate. She'd invited Graham for supper, although neither of them had done much justice to the meal, and she wondered if it would be easier if she was making coffee as she spoke.

Graham seemed to consider for a moment, and then he leaned across the table and took her hand. 'I can see you're upset,' he said gently. 'And if there's anything I can do you only have to tell me. But, Fliss, my dear, I have to be seen to be objective. However much I love you, we can't continue as before.'

'I know that.' Fliss sniffed. 'But you do still love me, don't you?'

Graham stared at her. 'How could you doubt it?'

'Well, I've hardly seen you since—since I got the news about Morgan.' She bit her lip. 'If only Aunt Sophie were here, I wouldn't feel so horribly isolated. As it is, I feel as if I'm living in some kind of vacuum.'

'Oh, Fliss!'

'I do love you, Graham.' She paused. 'You know that, don't you?'

'Well, I hoped so,' he admitted rather ruefully. Then he heaved a heavy sigh. 'Oh, Fliss, it's been hard for me, too. I've been trying to do my job when all the time I've been wondering how you were.'

'I've been better.' Fliss expelled a breath. 'He—Morgan, that is—he was so aggressive. We were like strangers with one another, Graham. I knew it would be hard seeing him again, but I had no idea how difficult it was going to be.'

Graham squeezed her fingers. 'I shouldn't say it, I know, but I am relieved.' He grimaced. 'I was sure you were going to tell me that you'd realised how much you loved your husband, after all. That was why I was so reluctant to come here. I was putting off what I saw as the evil day.'

Fliss felt a little of the tension she had been feeling ease. 'So you're not angry with me, then?'

'Angry with you?' Graham looked stunned. 'How could I be angry with you? I love you, Fliss. But I accepted weeks ago, when you first heard the news, that our relationship would have to be put on hold for a while, and you've no idea how good it feels to know that you still want to marry me.'

Fliss blinked back the tears that filled her eyes. 'Oh, Graham,' she said mistily. 'You're so good for me. With you, I feel—I feel—secure.' She had been going to say safe, but she decided Graham might not like the implication. It might look as if she thought Morgan was dangerous, and no man liked to be compared in that way.

'Anyway,' continued Graham cheerfully, 'I'm sure you realise that my role in the community means that we must practise a certain amount of caution—' He chuckled. 'The bishop wouldn't approve of our continuing our friendship as things are. But the church does provide many opportunities for us to spend time together, and it's not as if we've ever—well, made the mistake of anticipating our vows.'

Fliss hunched her shoulders. She knew Graham was right, but that didn't stop her wishing that they had become lovers when they'd had the chance. Perhaps if they'd shared that intimacy she wouldn't be feeling so empty. Or so apprehensive of what Morgan's return might mean.

'I must say, I'm glad we live in such a backwater,' Graham added. 'So far, we haven't been troubled by the media, although I suppose if your husband comes here we may find them nosing around.' He saw Fliss's expression and hurried to reassure her. 'Well, it's not as if we've got anything to hide. No one can blame you for trying to find happiness with someone else.' He hesitated. 'Not when you believed your husband was dead.'

'No.' Fliss shuddered. 'He—that is, Morgan—said there was no way he could have let us know he was alive.'

'Yes, and I read, just the other day, that he and Julius Mdola were friends,' Graham remarked thoughtfully. 'I must say, I find that part very hard to believe.'

'What? That they were friends?'

'No. That—that Morgan couldn't get in touch with you.'

'They were in a remote part of Africa, Graham; not a backwater in England.' Fliss found herself defending her husband. 'And although Morgan knew Mdola he certainly wasn't his friend.'

'Even so, there must have been some way of communicating with the outside world—'

Fliss stiffened. 'Are you calling him a liar?'

'No.' Graham looked embarrassed now. 'I'm just trying to justify my feelings, I suppose.' He sighed. 'Oh, Fliss, this is such an awful situation. Forgive me if I seem unsympathetic, but I can't help wishing that—that—'

'That Morgan was still dead?' she enquired tautly, and Graham made an involuntary sign of the cross.

'Oh, no,' he protested, but Fliss found his denial less than convincing. 'I meant, it would be easier if we could blame Morgan for allowing us to hope—to believe—' He broke off. 'You know what I mean, I'm sure.'

Tell me about it, thought Fliss grimly, realising they hadn't even scratched the surface of the problem yet. Her broken relationship with Graham was just the half of it. She dreaded what would happen when Morgan left the base.

'Anyway,' Graham continued, 'I haven't even asked how he is. That was most remiss of me. The poor man must be finding returning to England after so long something of an ordeal. I assume, as you came back alone, that he's staying with his parents for the time being.'

'Oh, no.' Fliss shook her head. 'Morgan's still at Craythorpe.'

'At the air force base?' Graham frowned. 'Whatever for?'

'For the reasons you've just mentioned,' said Fliss reluctantly. 'I suppose he is finding coming back quite an ordeal. There are doctors at the base who are experts at assessing his mental and physical fitness. He's very tense, I know that. I suppose he could be suffering from PTS.'

'PTS?'

Graham looked blank now and Fliss hid the surge of exasperation she felt. 'Post-traumatic stress,' she explained patiently, wondering at his naïvety. 'After all, Morgan has spent the last four years in strict confinement.' She hesitated. 'He probably lived in fear for his life.'

'Oh, do you think so?'

Graham sounded so doubtful that Fliss grew impatient despite herself. She wondered what he thought it was like to live with rebels, however friendly they might be. It was easy to be pragmatic in the comfort of your own home; less so when your comrades carried kalashnikovs to bed.

But, 'I think so,' was her only response, and as if sensing her feelings he tried to make amends.

'I'm sure Morgan understood the situation so much better than we do,' he declared, putting his napkin aside and pulling a wry face. 'So—how did his parents cope? Was it terribly awkward for them?'

Awkward?

Fliss's teeth dug into her lower lip as she strove to contain her frustration. 'Morgan's mother and father?' she said slowly, to give herself time to think. 'Well, yes. I believe they coped very well.'

'But you found him—aggressive,' Graham reminded her carefully. 'Didn't the Rikers find the same changes in their son?'

'Oh.' Fliss hesitated. 'Well, they weren't there all the time. I spoke to Morgan alone the following day.'

'He didn't—strike you, did he?' Apprehending her reluctance to continue, Graham gazed at her with some concern.

'No. It wasn't like that.' Fliss felt awkward. 'I—Morgan would never strike me.' Or would he? Did she really know her husband any more?

'Then what was it like?'

Graham was waiting to hear her explanation, and, realising she had to say something, Fliss got to her feet and turned her head away. 'I—just don't know what he's thinking,' she said, taking the easy way out. 'I don't know what he expects me to do.'

'Oh, Fliss.' Graham got up now, covering the space between them in a couple of strides. 'It sounds to me as if he might be ashamed of what happened. Why else would he get angry with you?'

'I don't know.' Fliss shook her head, feeling ashamed of herself for misleading him. 'Um—perhaps it was my fault.' She should have told him it was what she had said that had caused the rift between them. 'I was so nervous, I probably said the wrong thing.'

'You mustn't blame yourself.' Graham seemed to hesitate for a moment, and then he gave in to the urge to pull her into his arms. He was trembling; she could feel it; and she guessed he would regret this in the morning. His lips brushed her temple. 'I want you to promise me you won't let him frighten you again.'

Fliss clung to him eagerly, but she didn't make any promises she might not be able to keep. Morgan did frighten her, but there was nothing she could do about it. But she wished she'd have Graham's support when Morgan came back.

'When will I see you again?' she asked instead, and Graham drew back to look into her face.

'Whenever you like,' he said. 'You can always find me at the vicarage. With Mrs Arnold as chaperon, I don't think anyone could object.'

Fliss sighed impatiently. 'I don't mean at the vicarage,' she said. 'I meant, when can we spend an evening together again?'

'Oh, Fliss.' Graham's hands sought her shoulders now, and he stepped back so that she was at arm's length. 'I don't think we should do this again, my dear. Not until your marriage to Morgan has been dissolved.'

'Graham!'

'I'm sorry, Fliss.' He looked discomfited. 'But, I have to admit, the bishop has already spoken to me on this matter. I've assured him our relationship has ended—at least for the time being,' he appended hurriedly. 'You know how careful people in public life have to be these days.'

Fliss's shoulders sagged. 'But it could be—years before my marriage to Morgan is dissolved, as you put it,' she protested.

'Oh, I think not.' Graham released her and held out his hands to the flames leaping in the hearth. 'In a few weeks— if and when it becomes obvious that your marriage to Morgan isn't going to work—you can get a separation. And who will blame you, if you eventually get a divorce?'

Only Morgan—and Morgan's parents, thought Fliss wryly, wondering if Graham really believed his own words. Even he couldn't think it was going to be that easy. How could she ask Morgan for her freedom when he'd only just regained his?

Graham left a few minutes later, and although Fliss knew he was probably right to be cautious she wished he weren't quite so devoted to the church. It was only half-past nine, and she would have liked him to have stayed longer. Since she'd returned from Craythorpe, the evenings had seemed very long indeed.

But she'd known, even before she'd asked him when they were going to see one another again, that Graham would do nothing to jeopardise his position in the community, and since the end of their engagement he'd spent more and more time working for the church. He'd been neglecting his parishioners, he'd declared, when she'd commented on his rectitude. He'd even made a point of telling everyone that they remained friends in spite of everything. Friends!

Fliss closed the door behind him and leaned back against it with a heavy heart. She should be grateful that Morgan was alive, she thought unhappily, but all she could think about was the fact that just a few weeks ago she and Graham had been planning their wedding. Was it so unreasonable to feel apprehensive of what was to come?

Morgan Riker's wife. That was what she was: Morgan Riker's wife. She grimaced. For the last four years she'd been calling herself Morgan Riker's widow. She could hardly remember what it was like to be a wife.

She'd been shattered when Morgan had disappeared, of course. Hearing about the ambush and the burnt-out car, she'd suffered agonies, and there had been times when she hadn't wanted to carry on. If it hadn't been for Morgan's parents, and the fact that they had depended so much on her during those first few months, she might have been tempted to put an end to her own life. Her love for Morgan had been all-consuming. There hadn't been any room in her life for anything else.

To begin with, she'd stayed on in the house she and Morgan had bought in Kensington. She'd been teaching at a school close by, and it had seemed the most sensible thing to do. But the mortgage repayments were steep, and there were other expenses, and her salary simply wasn't enough. She'd also begun to feel haunted, living in the house that she and Morgan had shared. It held so many memories. She used to cry herself to sleep most nights.

When her aunt Sophie had mentioned that there was a job available at the school in Whittersley, it had seemed like the answer to her prayers. She was sorry to move further away from the Rikers, of course, and Celia had protested bitterly. But in the end they'd given her their blessing, even if her mother-in-law had never stopped complaining about how out of the way Whittersley was.

And Fliss had never expected to find happiness when she moved. Just an escape from the painful memories of the past. But she was happy in Whittersley; she enjoyed teaching at the village school. And, thanks to Graham, she had this cottage, and the friendship of one of the dearest men she'd ever known.

Or was ever likely to know, she thought fiercely. Just because Morgan had come back into her life, that didn't mean her feelings for Graham would ever change. He'd been there when she needed him; he'd helped her come to terms with Morgan's loss. He'd taught her that love came in many forms, and that the tempestuous relationship she had shared with Morgan was not necessarily the sweetest love of all.

The trouble was, like it or not, Morgan's return had caused an element of frenzy to re-enter her life. She'd continued to work this week, but she'd lived in fear of the school being invaded by the press. Seeing all the cameras at Craythorpe had reminded her of what it had been like when Morgan disappeared. For weeks, she'd had to cope with their intrusion into her life and her grief, and it was not something she wanted to have to live through again.

She slept badly, awakening the next morning with a thumping headache and an unpleasant taste in her mouth. She guessed it was the wine she'd drunk after Graham's departure that was responsible. He only ever had one glass with his supper, and Fliss had emptied the bottle last night before she'd gone to bed.

She was sipping her third cup of black coffee when she heard the rattle of the letterbox. It was too early for the mail, and she guessed it was the morning newspaper. But since she and the Rikers had visited Morgan at Craythorpe and found their own pictures occupying the front pages of most of the tabloids the following day she'd viewed subsequent editions with a slightly jaundiced eye.

However, assuming she had nothing to fear this morning, she stirred herself almost automatically and went into the hall to pick up the paper from the mat. She was holding her breath, as usual, but a swift glance at the front page reassured her. The current outbreak of food poisoning in the Midlands was still making the headlines.

Breathing a sigh of relief, she returned to her stool at the breakfast bar and poured herself another cup of coffee. She felt as if her nerves were running on caffeine at the moment, but the stimulant helped to get her through the day.

As she wasn't interested in the food-poisoning story—

she could only feel sympathy for the man who owned the restaurant where the outbreak was believed to have started—she laid the newspaper down and turned to the next page. A scantily clad model occupied page three, and although she had no desire to make an exhibition of herself in that way she couldn't help envying the woman her confidence.

These days, she was much more conscious of her own appearance. As Graham's fiancée, she had had to curb any temptation to wear short skirts or tight trousers outside the house. He loved her, but she could imagine his horror if she embarrassed him in any way. So far as Graham was concerned, sex and marriage were indivisible. He'd have been horrified if she'd confessed that she and Morgan had lived together for over a year before they'd tied the knot.

But Morgan wasn't like Graham, she reminded herself impatiently. Graham would never understand why Morgan hadn't wanted to wait until they were married before climbing into her bed. Or rather she'd climbed into his, she remembered guiltily. She'd been as eager as Morgan to satisfy the urgent needs she'd had.

And, anyway, that was lust, she chided herself irritably. It bore no resemblance to the feelings she and Graham had for one another. Theirs was a meeting of minds, a spiritual union—or so Graham liked to tell her. If she sometimes wished he were more adventurous in his approach, that was a flaw in her character, not his.

Nevertheless, she couldn't deny that thinking about sex with Morgan was still a turn-on. In the early days of their relationship, they hadn't been able to get enough of one another, and she recalled some of the places where they'd made love with some disbelief now. Like the time he'd invited her to go skinny-dipping on a holiday in California, and then taken her with the Pacific ocean adding its own rhythm to his powerful possession of her body...

A wave of heat swept over her at the images these

thoughts evoked, and, dismissing such wanton memories from her mind, she hurriedly turned to the next page. And found herself confronting a picture of herself and Graham at the cottage doorway, with the headline HOSTAGE'S RETURN MEANS HEARTACHE FOR VILLAGE VICAR occupying centre page.

Fliss's jaw dropped. 'Oh, God!' she mouthed silently, her eyes swiftly scanning the article that accompanied it. In essence, it described how Morgan Riker's return from the dead had had mixed blessings for the Reverend Graham Bland and his erstwhile bride-to-be.

Mixed blessings!

Fliss groaned. The deliberate imagery was repeated throughout the damning piece. It was full of pious quotations taken from the bible, with Graham's devotion to the woman he loved and had hoped to marry evident in every line.

She was horrified. It was exactly the kind of publicity Graham had been afraid of, and she realised that the picture must have been taken as he was leaving the night before. But how? And by whom? Neither of them had been aware of a third party being present. But then, Graham had been too concerned that they should present nothing more than a casual image, and she thanked her lucky stars that she hadn't given in to the impulse to bestow a goodnight kiss on his cheek.

She expelled an unsteady breath. How had they found her? How had they found Graham? It wasn't as if it was one of the local papers. The *Herald* was a national daily with a circulation to rival any of its competitors in the field.

Perhaps someone had informed on them. It wasn't as if her relationship with Graham had been a secret, and it was exactly the kind of story the tabloids loved to exploit. It was no use now wishing she hadn't insisted on Graham's joining her for supper the night before. She had the feeling that, with or without that picture, the story would have been published.

She carried her coffee mug to the sink and poured its contents down the drain. In truth, she was feeling a little sick, and she sensed she would need all her wits about her to handle the problems this could create.

She was checking she had everything she was likely to need for work when the phone rang. Immediately, her nerves kicked in, and she stood for several seconds staring at the machine before going to pick up the receiver.

'Yes?'

She spoke faintly, but Graham—how had she known it would be Graham?—heard her. 'Fliss? Fliss, is that you?'

Fliss took a deep breath. 'Who else?' she answered, with deliberate insouciance. 'Yes, it's me. I was just on my way out the door.' That was an exaggeration, but Graham was not to know that, and at least it put a limit on the time she had to talk.

But Graham wasn't interested in her schedule. 'Haven't you looked at the *Herald* this morning?' he demanded, half hysterically, and Fliss wondered if she dared feign ignorance.

However, deciding that would be sneaky, not to say spineless, she adopted a rueful tone. 'Well, yes. Yes, I have,' she admitted ruefully. 'Oh, darling, I don't know what to say.'

'You can start by not calling me *darling*!' exclaimed Graham passionately, and she realised he was in real danger of breaking down. 'Dear Lord, they may have your phone bugged. Have you thought of that?'

'Oh, Graham—'

'I mean it.' He took a strangled breath. 'How did they get that picture? Did you give it to them? I don't even remember when it was—'

'Of course I didn't give it to them!' Fliss found she resented the hint that she might have been to blame for what had happened, even if she was. 'They must have taken it as you were leaving last night.'

'Last night!' Graham was appalled. 'You mean, you think someone was hiding behind the hedge, waiting to snap me as soon as I came out of the cottage?'

'Well, maybe.' Fliss found she didn't like the idea of someone hanging around outside her house much either. 'Who knew you were coming to the cottage last night?'

Graham gasped. 'You can't mean that you think that someone—one of my parishioners—would inform the press of my intentions.'

'Who knows?' Fliss was as puzzled as he was. 'And it might not have been a *Herald* photographer who took the picture. It could have been someone from the local rag, hoping to make a killing.'

'A killing!' Graham had calmed down a bit now. 'I wish you wouldn't use those awful expressions, Fliss. Well, whoever it was, I think it's criminal.' His voice quivered with indignation. 'I knew I should have refused your invitation, but you were so sure there was no harm in us having a meal together—'

'And there wasn't,' protested Fliss. 'Don't let's lose sight of what's important here. It's not as if our relationship is a secret.'

'*Was*,' said Graham fiercely. 'Was a secret. As far as the bishop's concerned, we no longer have a relationship. I wish you'd remember that. What's he going to say when he sees this picture in the paper?'

Fliss sighed. 'Perhaps he doesn't take the *Herald*,' she said facetiously, but Graham was not amused.

'Whether he does or not, someone's bound to point it out to him.' He blew out a breath. 'I'm going to have to go and see him. If I can tell him that you needed my pastoral advice, I might just defuse any fall-out from the article itself.'

'But we didn't do anything wrong.' Fliss could feel herself getting annoyed. 'Graham, having supper with someone, whether she's married or not, does not constitute a denial of your faith.'

'I know that.' Graham made an obvious effort to regain his composure. 'But you have to admit that the content of the article is distasteful. It implies that I'm hoping we can renew our—our affair!'

'Well, aren't you?' Fliss spoke coolly, and then wished she hadn't when she heard his anguished protest. 'Oh, Graham,' she added softly, 'this is foolish. Vicars are human, just like everyone else.'

She could hear his uneven breathing, and sensed he was striving to regain control. 'You're probably right,' he said at last. 'I am overreacting. But His Lordship is so puritanical, as you well know.'

Fliss did know. Bishop Leonard had lost no time in informing her that, as a vicar's wife, certain standards of behaviour had to be upheld. He hadn't elaborated on what he meant, but his message was clear. As Mrs Bland, she was vulnerable, and any decline in moral conduct on her part would result in dire consequences for her husband.

'Look, I've got to go,' she said, realising that if she didn't get a move on she was going to be late for school prayers. Which wouldn't do her any good either. 'I'll speak to you later.' She paused. 'Try not to worry, hmm?'

'I'll try.' Graham did not sound optimistic, but she couldn't afford to spend any more time placating him now. 'And you will be careful what you say in future, won't you?' he appended, causing her to tighten her jaw. 'I don't want any unwary comments appearing in tomorrow's paper.'

CHAPTER FIVE

As FLISS had expected, the article caused a few comments during the course of the day. Susan Petrie, the close friend she had at the school, was sympathetic, but most of her colleagues were amused by the sentiments expressed. They all knew Graham from scout parties and coffee mornings as well as in his role as the local vicar. And they seemed to find the idea of him being heartbroken more humorous than sad.

Even so, Fliss was glad when the bell rang at the end of the afternoon, and the class she had been taking—eight-year-olds, who were more interested in whether the school hamster was pregnant again or not than in their teacher's affairs—scrambled for the door. It was Friday, and they were exuberant, looking forward to the weekend. It seemed a millennium since she had been that age, Fliss thought enviously. Oh, to be young and irresponsible again.

'Going anywhere tomorrow?' asked Susan as she and Fliss emerged into the faintly frosty air of a March afternoon, and her companion sighed.

'I'm not sure.'

'What do you mean, you're not sure?'

Susan was puzzled, and Fliss gave a rueful sigh. 'Well, perhaps I ought to go and see Morgan again,' she brooded unhappily. 'I know the Rikers are going, so perhaps I ought to tag along.'

'Tag along!' Susan gave her a reproving look. 'Fliss, I'm sure you're the most important person in Morgan's life at the moment.'

'I doubt it.' Fliss shook her head, remembering the contempt in Morgan's eyes with a shiver of remorse. 'And if

59

it's true I don't think I want that responsibility. I know I may sound hard, but I've had four years to accept that that period of my life is over.'

'The period you spent with Morgan?'

'Yes.' Fliss tossed the end of her scarf over her shoulder. 'He was captured in 1995—or killed, as we thought then. I've had to make a life for myself alone. Well, until I met Graham, that is.'

'Hmm.' Susan was thoughtful. 'Well, I'm sorry it's happened this way, Fliss, but I can't help thinking that if it was Russ I'd be over the moon that he was coming home. Are you sure you're not letting Graham influence you? I remember how devastated you were when you first came here.'

'Well, I was devastated then,' said Fliss unhappily, and then stiffened when she saw a man standing by the school gates. He had a camera slung about his neck, and it seemed obvious that he was waiting for her. 'Oh, God, can you give me a lift, Sue? I think he's a reporter.'

'Who?' Susan looked blank at first, and then she too saw the stranger watching them. 'Oh, heavens!' she exclaimed. 'Of course I can. Do you think it's going to be like this from now on?'

'I hope not.' Fliss spoke fervently, folding herself into Susan's old Ford with a feeling of despair. 'I suppose if it goes on I'll have to borrow Aunt Sophie's Volvo. She said I could use it while she was away.'

'No problem.' Susan tucked an errant strand of curly blonde hair behind her ear and slipped behind the wheel. 'But it's obvious that article is going to engender some interest. I suppose you're hoping Morgan hasn't seen it.'

'Morgan!' Fliss gulped. Her anxieties had stretched to the Rikers, but no one else. 'You don't think that's likely, do you?' she added, deciding to phone her in-laws as soon as she got home.

'No, I suppose not.' Susan was reassuring, but Fliss

couldn't help feeling anxious as they drove out of the school yard. The thwarted reporter raised his camera as they drove past, but Fliss put a hand up to shade her face. That was one picture, she thought smugly, that he wouldn't be able to use.

'Anyway,' Susan went on as they drove the couple of hundred yards to Fliss's cottage, 'if things do get on top of you, you can always come and have a meal with us.'

'Thanks.' Fliss was grateful, but she had the feeling she'd be staying at home. And what was the point of going to Craythorpe if Morgan didn't want to see her?

The sight of several more reporters gathered at her gate was daunting, however. Even Susan looked dismayed as she brought the old car to a halt. 'Are you sure you'll be all right?' she asked worriedly as Fliss gathered together her belongings in preparation for getting out of the car.

'I'll survive,' said Fliss, with a slight smile, hoping she sounded more confident than she felt. So long as she didn't say anything, there was nothing they could do.

The men—and one woman, she noticed—all pressed forward as she slammed the car door, but somehow she managed to make it to the gate. The latch on the gate was stiff, and she had to jiggle it for a moment before it opened, but then an arm brushed past her shoulder, and a voice said, 'Let me.'

Fliss was furious. Beyond the gate was her property, and if they forced their way inside she intended to call the police. 'I can do it,' she said, brushing the man's hand aside and squeezing through the crack.

'I'm sure.'

The man's voice was harsh, but there was something unnervingly familiar about it. And, as she was registering this fact, he ignored her threat and followed her up the path.

'How dare—?' There was fury in her eyes as she turned to face him, but then her jaw sagged. 'Morgan,' she whispered in disbelief, and he scowled as she used his name.

'Wh-what are you doing here?' she stammered, too shocked to consider her words, and she heard the sudden stirring of interest behind her.

'Not here. Wait until we get inside,' he muttered irritably, and she hurried to insert her key in the lock. But her mind was buzzing with questions: how had he found his way here? Why had no one recognised him just now?

She answered that question herself. Once they were safely inside, and the blinds tipped to prevent any unwanted intrusion, her first real look at him solved her doubts. In black woollen trousers and a thick black parka, with the collar turned up about his beard-roughened features, he looked like one of them.

Or worse, she acknowledged tensely as she unbuttoned her overcoat and hung it away in the cupboard under the stairs. In fact, he looked quite disreputable, the stubble on his head giving him a tough appearance, and no one would have recognised him from the clean-cut photograph of the army officer his father had originally supplied to the press.

As she met his calculating gaze, Fliss knew without a shadow of a doubt that he'd seen the article in the *Herald*, too. Her concern about what the Rikers might think had been a mild thing in comparison to the anxiety she was feeling now.

'Have—have you been waiting long?' she asked, putting her bag down on the table, her eyes darting nervously about the room. 'Um—can I take your coat?' she added, belatedly aware that she was forgetting her manners, but Morgan shook his head and pushed his hands deeper into his pockets.

'I've been waiting a while,' he replied after a moment, standing in the middle of the floor, like some kind of avenging angel, she thought foolishly. Nevertheless, despite the fact that the room was warm, he looked chilled to the bone, and she remembered he was used to a much hotter climate than this.

'Would you like some tea?' she asked awkwardly, going into the kitchen without waiting to hear his reply. The newspaper that had caused such a fuss was still lying open on the bar where she'd left it that morning, and, folding it up, she stuffed it into the waste bin.

If Morgan was aware of what she was doing, he made no comment. He just turned to watch her through the open kitchen door. Her hands shook as she filled the kettle, and she hoped he didn't notice. His shoulders were hunched against the cold, and his stare was penetrating between his narrowed lids.

She wondered what he was thinking. Had he any idea how she felt? He looked so grim, he barely resembled the man she'd married at all. Of course, he was thinner, but that was to be expected, but his lack of hair gave him a sinister look.

He'd never been a handsome man, she conceded critically. His hard features possessed a piercing intelligence, but that was all. Nevertheless, she remembered, with some reluctance, that that hadn't stopped women from being attracted to him, and he still retained that sensual appeal.

'Does—does anyone know you're here?' she asked impulsively, and then realised how unguarded her words had been. They seemed to imply that she had doubts about his mental capacity. That he was some kind of inmate who'd escaped detention.

'I mean,' she corrected herself hurriedly, 'do—do your parents know what you're doing?'

Morgan didn't answer her for a moment. Then he said softly, 'How else would I have known where to come? You omitted to tell me that you'd sold our house.' His jaw tightened. 'Is there anything else I should know?'

Fliss chose not to answer that. 'I—I didn't forget to tell you about the house,' she said, swallowing. 'We just didn't get around to—to things like that.'

'No.'

Morgan's tone was sardonic, and she felt a glimmer of indignation. 'I couldn't afford to go on paying the mortgage,' she told him defensively. 'And besides, I wanted to—to get away.'

'From me?'

'From memories of you, yes,' she answered truthfully. 'I'd been told you were dead. I couldn't go on living in that house alone.'

'And that's the real reason you sold the house?'

'No, I've told you, I couldn't afford the mortgage. My salary just wasn't enough.'

'And what about the book? My book. The book that was waiting to be published. Surely that earned something more than the initial advance? Marius Blake was fairly enthusiastic, as I recall.'

Fliss sighed. 'The book was never published.'

Morgan looked taken aback. 'Why not?'

'Oh—I don't know. After you were—believed killed, the publishers offered one excuse after another. There was some dispute over revisions or something.'

Morgan scowled. 'In other words, they reneged on the agreement?'

'Perhaps.' Fliss could still recall how distraught she'd felt at that time. 'Anyway, I was in no fit state to argue with them. It all seemed so morbid, somehow.'

Morgan inclined his head. 'So you came here?'

'Yes.'

'Why?'

'Why?' Fliss stared at him. 'Well, because of the job, I suppose.' She hesitated. 'And because of the availability of this cottage.'

'But whose idea was it?' he persisted. 'Why would you move so far away from town? I can accept that you'd want to leave the house and, possibly, London. But Whittersley isn't exactly the first place that springs to mind.'

Fliss began setting cups and saucers on a tray. 'It was

my decision,' she said firmly. 'Do you still take milk and sugar?'

'I don't care.' Morgan regarded her stonily. 'Why didn't you try to get a job in Sussex instead? You could have stayed with Mum and Dad at Tudor Cross.'

'I don't think so.' Fliss took a deep breath. 'Much as I like your mother and father, I wouldn't want to live with them.'

'Why not?' Morgan came to fill the kitchen doorway, propping his shoulder against the jamb. 'It seems a more sensible solution. Unless you had a more personal reason for moving here.'

A more personal reason.

Her belief that Morgan had seen the article in the *Herald* seemed well founded. Whether his parents had seen it first and told him about it didn't really matter. The fact was, that was the real reason he had left the base.

'Aunt Sophie told me about the job, if that's what you mean,' she declared abruptly, knowing full well that that wasn't what he'd meant at all. 'She told me about the job, and she mentioned that this cottage might be available to rent. I jumped at the chance. Decent unfurnished accommodation is hard to find.'

Morgan's scowl had deepened now, but she refused to be daunted by his mood. The kettle was nearly boiling, and she spooned tea into the teapot. If only Aunt Sophie were here. She could have done with her support.

'And that's the only reason you chose to come and live in this backwater?'

'Yes.' Fliss made the tea with a decidedly unsteady hand. And then, because she was weary of prevaricating, she said, 'It was nothing to do with Graham Bland, if that's what you're trying to say.'

'Graham Bland?'

The way he said Graham's name, as if he'd never heard it before, made Fliss want to scream. It might be four years since they'd lived together, but she knew him too well. He was deliberately trying to lead her into a trap.

'Yes, Graham Bland,' she said, trying to keep her voice from wobbling as she picked up the tray. 'The Reverend Graham Bland, if you want to be formal. The vicar of St Margaret's here in the village, and a—a very good friend of mine.'

Morgan's nostrils flared. 'More than a good friend, surely,' he remarked, and she was surprised at the civility of his tone. But when she met his eyes a shiver caused goosebumps to feather her flesh. Their expression was chilling: a mixture of anger and raw savagery she'd never seen before.

'You've read the article,' she said, through tight lips, wishing he would move out of the way so that she could carry the tray into the other room.

'Did you think I wouldn't?' he countered, his gaze skimming over the copper pans that hung above the counter and the potted fern she had suspended by a hook from the beamed ceiling before returning to her face. 'Why did you let me think you were—pleased to have me back?'

Fliss licked her dry lips. 'I am pleased—'

'Are you?' Patently, he didn't believe her. 'And, come to think of it, I should have suspected something was wrong. A wife doesn't usually flinch from her husband's touch.'

'I didn't!'

'Didn't you?' Morgan gave her one more damning look before moving away from the door. 'You were scared to be alone with me. I don't blame you. With that on your conscience it must have been quite an ordeal.'

'It wasn't like that.'

Fliss followed him with the tray, and Morgan turned to give her a scornful stare. 'It was just like that,' he told her flatly. 'Was that what you really came back to say?'

'No.' Fliss deposited the tray with some relief on the

coffee table. 'I wouldn't—that is—I had no intention of discussing my—my association with Graham.'

'So when were you going to tell me?' he demanded, regarding her enquiringly. 'Before or after you told me about the house?'

Fliss could feel her pulses racing. During the weeks since she'd learned that Morgan was alive, she'd tried several times to imagine what she was going to say to him. The truth was, she admitted guiltily, if the article hadn't been published, she didn't know when she'd have told him. Or even if. It would have been so much easier if she'd had the chance to spend some time with him; to prove that their relationship wasn't going to work.

'Wh-why don't you sit down?' she suggested, knowing she would feel better if he wasn't towering over her. She gestured towards the sofa, but Morgan didn't move an inch.

'How long?' he asked harshly, and Fliss, meeting his accusing eyes, felt an uneasy quivering in her bones.

'How long—what?' she asked, trying to sound as if she didn't understand him, and Morgan's mouth compressed against his teeth.

'Don't play games with me, Fliss,' he advised her coldly. 'You know precisely what I mean. How long did you intend to wait until you told me? How long before you replaced me with this—this parson? Whose heart has apparently been broken by my return from the dead?'

Fliss took a steadying breath. 'Graham hasn't replaced you.'

'Hasn't he?' Morgan gave her another contemptuous look.

'No.' She straightened her spine. 'He—he's the vicar, as I've told you. We've been friends since I moved to Whittersley, I suppose.'

'Friends?'

'To begin with, yes.' Fliss gained a little more confidence in telling the truth. 'He's a governor of the school where I

work, and the church owns this cottage. He—he was there
when I needed a friend, and he helped me get my life back
together.'

'I'll bet.'

Morgan was sarcastic now, and, realising they weren't
going to resolve anything by standing arguing with one
another, Fliss perched on the edge of a chair and leaned
towards the tray. But before she could pour the tea
Morgan's hand descended on her nape, and the pot clattered
noisily, spilling tea all over the cloth.

'I just want you to know that as far as I'm concerned
you're still my wife,' he told her harshly, his narrow fingers
digging into her neck. 'And if that bastard so much as lays
a hand on you he'll have me to deal with. I know what
these pilgrims are like, taking advantage of vulnerable
women—'

'Graham didn't take advantage of me!' Fliss exclaimed
fiercely, getting up from the chair and nearly overturning
the table in the process. She was barely aware of what she
was doing, only of the desire to put as much space between
them as possible. 'Don't touch me,' she cried, brushing her
hand across the spot where his fingers had gripped her.
'Just—don't—touch me! Do you hear?'

'Why not?' Morgan wasn't at all intimidated by her
trembling warning. 'You are still my wife, aren't you? You
didn't go and get a divorce while I wasn't here to defend
myself.'

'Of course not.' Fliss stared at him with contemptuous
eyes. 'My God, have you forgotten already? I thought you
were dead!'

'Ah, yes.' But Morgan didn't sound repentant. 'You
didn't need to get a divorce. Off with the old, and on with
the new.'

'You don't understand.' Fliss wished this wasn't happening. 'Graham and I have been friends for over three
years—long before—before we discovered we—cared

about one another. You're behaving as if I started going out with other men the minute I got the news.'

His brows, which were several shades darker than his hair, arched assessingly. 'I only have your word that you didn't.'

'It's the truth.' She gazed at him with something akin to anguish in her eyes. 'You should know I wouldn't lie to you,' she added painfully. 'I don't think you're giving my feelings a second thought.'

'Perhaps not.' Morgan regarded her consideringly now, and then lifted his shoulders in a careless shrug. 'But you have to admit you've been somewhat less than frank in what you've told me. I get the feeling you wish I had died in that ambush. My coming back has created problems for you.'

'That's not true.' Fliss was indignant. 'But you can't deny you didn't consider my feelings when you went away. You didn't have to go, Morgan, and you know it. But you let Paul Giles persuade you there was no danger.'

'Paul Giles.' Morgan said the man's name with more warmth than he'd shown thus far. Then his eyes darkened. 'So that's what this is all about: you blame me for what happened.' He shook his head. 'You never did like Paul, of course.'

Fliss had no intention of getting into that. Her opinion that Paul Giles had always taken advantage of every situation had only been strengthened in the weeks after Morgan had disappeared. He was another reason why she'd been so willing to leave London. His insinuation that he might be of assistance to her now had left her shocked, and trembling with indignation.

She sighed and then, with a nervous hand, she urged him to sit down. 'Can't we talk about this like civilised human beings?' she pleaded. 'You can't have expected that things would stay the way they were.'

Morgan pulled a hand out of his pocket, but although

she flinched all he did was rake his fingers across his stubbled scalp. 'I don't know what I expected,' he replied heavily. He glanced around. 'I don't suppose you have anything to drink?'

'Well, the tea's—'

'Not tea,' he interjected harshly. 'Don't you have any spirits? Or a beer? They've been pumping me full of tea since I got off the plane.'

'Oh.' Fliss twisted her hands together. 'Well, there may be some whisky left over from Christmas.' And then, aware of his narrow-eyed enquiry, she added, 'Your father brought it with him when he and your mother came for a visit.'

'Sounds good to me.'

She hesitated. 'But aren't you on medication?' she faltered. 'I'm not sure that alcohol is quite—'

'Just get it,' said Morgan flatly, at last obeying her wishes and subsiding onto the sofa. He loosened his coat. 'At least it's a bit warmer in here.'

Fliss delayed as long as she dared, and then went into the kitchen. She noticed Morgan cast a sardonic look at a photograph of Fliss and himself that his mother had brought and which Fliss had placed on the mantelpiece, before slumping back against the cushions and closing his eyes. Taking the whisky out of the cupboard, she studied it doubtfully. She wished now she'd never admitted she had the stuff.

'Morgan...' she began again, hovering in the doorway, but he didn't even bother to turn his head.

'I'm waiting,' he said grimly, and, feeling frustrated, she collected a glass from the china cabinet that stood just inside the living-room door.

'It's your funeral,' she muttered, thrusting them both at him, and then went scarlet when she realised what she'd said.

'You wish,' he retorted, and she blew out a breath in

some despair. He was so pale; coming here must have exhausted him. She was amazed that his parents had allowed him to travel alone.

He looked at her as he unscrewed the bottle, and she found herself getting hot and bothered under his steady gaze. They might be virtual strangers to one another now, but they had once shared every intimacy, and when he splayed his legs to reach for the glass she had to force herself to look away.

'Sit down,' he said, almost as if it were his house, and although she resented his assumption of authority she was glad to take the weight off her legs. In fact, she was feeling decidedly unsteady. Crossing swords with Morgan had never been easy. Unlike Graham, he made no concessions because of her sex.

She perched on the edge of the chair opposite, knees pressed tightly together, hands linked loosely in her lap. But she didn't relax; her nerves were too jumpy. She didn't know what he expected of her. She was half afraid he was still spoiling for a fight.

'Aren't you going to join me?' he asked, pouring a generous measure of whisky into his glass, and then taking a reckless gulp. She wondered if he'd forgotten how strong malt whisky was. How long had it been since he'd had a drink?

She thought he was going to choke. The raw spirit caught the back of his throat, and it was several seconds before he could even get his breath. She jumped to her feet and went to thump on his back, and he burst into a hoarse bout of coughing. He was clutching his throat with his free hand and silently begging for some relief.

For a moment Fliss didn't know what to do, but then she hurried into the kitchen for a glass of water. Taking the whisky glass from him, she replaced it with the tumbler, and he gulped the water gratefully, as soon as he could breathe again.

It was some minutes before he attempted to speak and when he did his voice was rough and raw with pain. 'Okay, you were right,' he said. 'Maybe I will pass on the whisky.' He heaved a breath. 'D'you have a soft drink of some kind? My throat feels as if it's been cut.'

'Of course.'

Fliss hurried into the kitchen again and returned with a can of orange juice and another glass. But Morgan merely flicked the tab and drank thirstily from the can itself, the unhealthy colour in his face subsiding as his breathing returned to normal.

'Right,' he said, when his throat felt easier, flopping back against the cushions again with the almost empty can balanced on his chest. 'At least you know you've got nothing to fear from me. As you can see I'm still as weak as a bloody kitten.'

A kitten, bloody or otherwise, did not come to Fliss's mind when she looked at Morgan. An injured cat perhaps, and not of the domestic variety either. His eyes were too wary, the danger in them muted now, but still lurking behind his sardonic gaze. She shouldn't lose sight of the fact that his claws hadn't been blunted. They were simply sheathed at the moment to enhance the image he wanted to portray.

'Are you hungry?' she asked, aware that she was looking for an excuse to go out of the room again, and Morgan gave her a knowing look.

'I thought you wanted to talk,' he said. 'Or have you changed your mind?' His eyes narrowed. 'Unless you're hungry, of course.'

Hungry!

Fliss felt as if her throat had closed up and she'd never be able to eat again. 'I can wait,' she said, aware that it was barely half-past four. She glanced towards the windows. 'How long do you think those people will stay outside the cottage?'

'Who knows?' Morgan's voice was cool. 'Why? Are you expecting your boyfriend to call?'

'I don't have a boyfriend,' she retorted, not altogether truthfully. 'I just don't like the idea of being observed.'

'Then close the curtains,' said Morgan wearily, but it was still daylight outside, and she didn't want to arouse any more curiosity about her affairs. 'Sit down,' he added, when it became obvious she wasn't going to do as he'd said. 'If I can stand the heat, so should you.'

Fliss sighed, but she eventually did as he'd said, gripping the arms of the chair with sweaty palms. She knew they had to talk, but she was still nervous. His coming here had thrown all her half-conceived notions to the winds.

'So...' Morgan regarded her coolly. 'How long ago was the picture I saw taken?'

'What picture?' she began uncertainly, casting a doubtful glance towards the mantelpiece. But then, meeting his sceptical assessment, she said, 'Oh—it was taken yesterday evening, as—as he was leaving.'

Morgan's nostrils flared. 'Yesterday evening?' he echoed. 'So this—boyfriend, who isn't a boyfriend, is still part of your life?'

'He's a friend,' she protested at once, hating to feel so defensive. 'It was the first evening we've spent together since we—since we learned you were still alive.'

'We?' Morgan's lips drew down bitterly. 'Have you any idea how cosy that sounds? *We* haven't spent an evening together since *we* learned that *you* were still alive. That's what you said. You're pairing yourself with him, not me.'

Fliss sighed. 'It was just how it came out.'

'Was it?' Morgan leaned back against the cushions, hooking an ankle across his knee. 'I wonder why you chose last night to renew your acquaintance and not some other? Could it be that you had the possible results of the photograph to discuss?'

'No.' Fliss was indignant now. 'I've told you, the photograph must have been taken last night. If you want to know why Graham was here, I'll tell you. It was to tell him about my trip to Craythorpe last weekend.'

Morgan's brows arched. 'You wanted to discuss what you were going to do about me, right?'

'No.' That was too close for comfort and Fliss found herself foundering for a reply. 'I—I just wanted to tell him that you—well, that you were staying at the base for the time being. He's a decent man; he wanted to know how you were.'

'I'll bet.'

'It's true.'

'It wasn't to advise him that the coast was clear if he should choose to take advantage of it?' Morgan grimaced. 'I'm sure—Graham—would jump at the chance of continuing your—affair.'

'It wasn't an affair!' exclaimed Fliss angrily. 'And you don't know Graham very well if you think he'd do a thing like that!'

'I don't know him at all,' Morgan reminded her drily. 'So tell me. Are you saying he doesn't have the same urges as the rest of us?'

Fliss caught her breath. 'Graham's a man of God,' she retorted shortly. 'He respects the laws of matrimony. He'd never do anything to betray his vows or mine.'

'You mean he's a prig,' said Morgan contemptuously. 'Either that, or you're a better liar these days than you used to be.'

'He's not a prig!' Fliss was mortified. 'He's an honest man; that's what he is.' She stiffened her spine. 'Perhaps that's not a concept you're familiar with. I don't know how often you lied to me before.'

'I never lied to you,' he snarled at once. 'But you have to admit there aren't many men like him around.'

'I know.' Fliss felt pleased that he'd acknowledged it.

'Unlike some of his contemporaries, he practises what he preaches.'

'A real paragon.' Morgan's tone was mocking nevertheless. 'So what does he preach? I assume you attend his church.'

'Well, yes.' Fliss faltered. 'He believes in the power of prayer, I suppose. That anything is possible if—if we have faith.'

'Even making love to another man's wife,' remarked Morgan sardonically, flexing his booted foot. 'Forgive me if I find his goodness hard to take.'

Fliss wouldn't rise to his bait. It was obvious he was never going to believe her, and she wished they could talk about something else. Like what had happened to him while she was trying to make another life for herself? She wished he would stop looking at her as if she'd betrayed him when she hadn't.

Her lips tightened, and she looked away from him. But she could still see his face in her mind's eye. He was pale, but his skin was darkly tanned in spite of it, and she was aware that it added to his sinister appeal.

When his hair grew back, he'd look much more familiar, she acknowledged. As it was, she couldn't help being intimidated by his threatening mien. Yet, when she noticed a curl of sun-bleached hair that had escaped the neckline of his woollen shirt, she couldn't deny it stirred unwelcome memories. She might not want to admit it, but the reality of him there, sitting on her sofa, caused the hair on the back of her neck to stand on end.

'So last night's get-together wasn't a romantic assignation?' he queried at last, crushing the empty can with evident satisfaction, and she wondered if he was imagining it was Graham's head.

'No,' she replied stiffly, even though an embarrassing wave of colour invaded her neck. 'I've told you: Graham and I are still friends, but that's all.'

'And you think that's any consolation?' he demanded harshly, tossing the can onto the table and leaning towards her across its width. 'For God's sake, Fliss, I want to know how well you knew the bastard. Before you tell me anything more about his unblemished character, I'd like to hear when you last slept with the guy!'

CHAPTER SIX

FLISS'S lips parted. It was on the tip of her tongue to tell him that she and Graham had never been to bed together, but his attitude—and her own unwelcome awareness of his masculinity—kept her silent. She didn't know when she might be grateful for that barrier between them. And, dammit, he had no right to ask her a question like that. All right, he was her husband—barely. But for the past four years she'd been forced to fend for herself.

So, 'You don't expect me to answer that,' she said instead, feeling only a little remorse for the spasm of pain that crossed his face at her words. 'I'm sorry you had to find out about—about Graham so bluntly. I intended to tell you myself, but—I didn't get the chance.'

'When?' Morgan rested his forearms along his parted thighs, his hands curling and uncurling with obvious frustration. 'I thought I knew you, Fliss, but I'm beginning to wonder. What other secrets are you keeping that I don't know anything about?'

'Nothing!' Fliss almost choked with indignation. 'I've got nothing to hide.'

'And I have?' Morgan challenged, with bitter humour. 'For pity's sake, don't you think I have a right to know who's been sleeping with my wife?'

Fliss gasped. 'You make it sound as if I've had a string of lovers,' she protested fiercely.

'And I only have your word that you haven't,' he countered, 'if that's what you're trying to say.'

'Well, I haven't,' said Fliss tautly, pressing her hands together. 'So stop trying to trick me. My—my relationship with Graham is nothing to do with you.'

'So you do have a relationship.'

'The relationship I *had* with Graham,' she amended hotly. 'Oh, you're getting me so confused, I don't know what I'm saying any more.'

'Perhaps that's one way I'll get at the truth,' he commented wryly.

'Well, you can please yourself what you believe,' she retorted. 'I don't have to defend myself to you.'

'So it's over?'

'Yes, it's over,' Fliss agreed tersely, wondering at the arbitrary way she'd dismissed the man she'd professed to love the night before. 'Now—can we talk about something else? Like, how did you get here? I'm surprised your parents let you come alone.'

'They didn't have a choice.'

'Why?' Fliss stared at him. 'I assume you told them what you planned to do.'

'I haven't seen my parents,' he replied flatly. 'I phoned them from London, that's all. After I'd found you didn't live in Chaucer Road.'

'But you said they'd given you my address.'

'So they did.'

'Then—'

'I let them think I wanted to write to you.'

Fliss caught her breath. 'So they don't know that you're here?'

'No.'

'Who does know, then?'

'You do.' Morgan's mouth compressed. 'And those guys outside may suspect something after the way you let me in.'

'But the doctor at the base—'

'Is probably sending out a search party.' And at her look of horror he said, 'I'm not a prisoner any longer, Fliss. They can't keep me at the base against my will.'

'So they know you're here?'

Morgan heaved a sigh. 'No. They think I'm in London. The address I gave them was the house in Chaucer Road.'

Fliss shook her head. 'So how did you get here?'

'I took a train from Paddington, like anyone else.'

'After taking a train from Ipswich to London?'

'Obviously.'

Fliss expelled a breath. 'You must have been travelling all day.'

'Since about ten-thirty, I guess,' he agreed equably. 'I was lucky enough to make a connection without too much delay.'

She got to her feet. 'So, have you had any lunch? Or is that a silly question? Honestly, Morgan, you're supposed to be looking after your health, not charging about the country.'

'Oh, please…' Morgan looked up at her wearily. 'Don't act as if my well-being means anything to you. You can't tell the husband you haven't seen for four years that I don't have the right to know if you're still sleeping with your lover, and then get upset because you think I've had nothing to eat!'

Fliss shook her head. 'That's so unfair.'

'Yeah.' Morgan was looking increasingly worn. 'Well, life is unfair, didn't you know? You don't suppose my spending the past four years in virtual isolation was a picnic, do you? Or coming back to find that my wife's been shacking up with someone else!'

'I haven't been—shacking up, as you put it, with anyone,' burst out Fliss painfully. 'All right, maybe I shouldn't have tried to hide it from you, but Graham and I—well, we haven't ever been lovers, and that's the truth.'

Morgan gazed at her contemptuously now, and she cringed a little at his expression. 'You know,' he said harshly, 'I still think you're lying through your teeth.'

Fliss blinked. 'You don't believe me?'

'No.' Morgan watched the colour in her face subside.

'You'd do anything to protect that sanctimonious son-of-a-bitch, wouldn't you? What's the matter? Are you afraid I'll knock his adulterous teeth down his adulterous throat?'

Fliss trembled. 'I'm not protecting him, Morgan. It's the truth.'

'Is it?' He dropped his gaze, but he didn't sound as if he believed her. 'Well, whatever.' He pressed his hands down on his thighs and got to his feet. 'I guess that's my cue to go.'

'To go?' Fliss was dismayed now. 'But you can't go. I mean—how will you get back to the base?'

'I'm not going back to the base,' said Morgan flatly. 'Not tonight anyway. I'll go to Tudor Cross instead.'

'But you can't.' Fliss was desperate. 'I mean—what are your mother and father going to think?' She glanced helplessly about her. 'Do you want them to think we're having problems already?' She swallowed. 'In any case, there are no buses to Salisbury after four o'clock.'

'I didn't come by bus. I got a cab,' said Morgan, attempting to fasten his parka. 'I guess I can get one back. Stop fussing, Fliss, it doesn't go with your new image. How does it feel to be unattached again?'

Fliss's jaw dropped. 'I'm not unattached.'

'No, but you might as well be.' Morgan seemed to retain some resentment after all. He looked up. 'You could always run me to the station yourself. Salisbury's only—what? About a dozen miles away?'

'Ten,' said Fliss stiffly. 'But I can't run you to the station, even if I wanted to. I don't have a car.'

Morgan scowled. 'You sold my car?'

'No.' Fliss held up her head. 'The finance company repossessed it.'

'You couldn't keep up the payments, I suppose?'

'That's right.' Fliss was defensive. 'I had a lot of—expenses. It was the least of my problems. I never used a car in town.'

'And when you came here?'

'It was an extravagance.' Fliss paused. 'Your father did offer to help me buy one, but I turned him down. It wasn't necessary, and I preferred to be independent. If I can't walk where I want to go, I get a lift or take the bus.'

'A lift?' Morgan's eyes darkened. 'From Graham, I presume.'

'From Aunt Sophie usually,' retorted Fliss, growing tired of this conversation. 'I had to stand on my own two feet. Can't you understand that?'

'What I understand is that you appear to have done everything you could to cut yourself off from my family,' he replied coldly. 'Was that before or after your boyfriend came on the scene?'

Fliss took a breath. 'Your parents don't know about—my friendship with Graham. Well, they do, but they don't know that he asked me to marry him.'

'I see.' Morgan's eyes narrowed. 'Oh, well—I guess they do by now.'

'They've seen the article, too?'

'I don't know. They didn't discuss it with me.' His lips twisted. 'Like you, they probably thought it wouldn't be the wisest thing to do.'

'Oh, please...' Fliss gazed at him pleadingly. 'Morgan, you can't just walk out again. Not like this.' A thought occurred to her. 'Not with those reporters outside. Do you want them to speculate in tomorrow's edition why you didn't stay the night?'

Morgan looked doubtful suddenly. 'Are you sure you're not just afraid of what my leaving would do to the venerable Graham's reputation?' he queried cynically. 'It's not my reputation you're worried about; it's his.'

Fliss could have denied it, but she guessed he wouldn't believe her. And anything was better than having his possible collapse on her conscience tonight.

'Well, maybe,' she conceded, praying it wouldn't work

against her. And there was no doubt that it wouldn't do
Graham's reputation any harm. 'Oh, Morgan, we have to
talk, and we can't do that if you walk out of here. Do you
want your parents to be hounded by the media, too?'

Morgan gave up trying to fasten his zip. 'What are you
suggesting?'

'That you stay here, of course.' Fliss issued the invitation, and then wondered how wise she was being in doing
so. But she had committed herself now, so she went on
doggedly, 'It's Saturday tomorrow. You can decide then
what you want to do.'

Morgan looked thoughtful. 'Well...'

'You know I'm right.' Fliss pressed her advantage. 'I'm
not working tomorrow, and—and I could always borrow
Aunt Sophie's car and take you where—wherever you want
to go.'

'Aunt Sophie.' Morgan's expression softened, and Fliss
guessed he was remembering her aunt. 'How is the old
girl?' he asked, with sudden interest. 'I wouldn't mind seeing her again before I leave.'

'Well, she's in Australia at the moment,' said Fliss re-
gretfully. 'She's visiting my cousin and her family, in New
South Wales. But she's due back in a couple of weeks and
I know she'd like to see you, too.' Now why had she said
that? 'She was delighted when I phoned and told her that
you were home.'

'Was she?'

Morgan's wry look was a gentle reminder that he didn't
believe her, and she hid her embarrassment by moving towards him and holding out her hand for his coat. 'Of course
she was,' she declared firmly as he gave in to her silent
demand and handed over the heavy parka. 'I'll hang this
up,' she added, 'and then I'll see what I've got in the
fridge.'

He could have refused. He could have insisted on keeping his coat on and made an awkward situation even worse.

He could even have grasped her wrist, she conceded unsteadily. How would she have felt if he'd pulled her into his arms?

But he didn't, of course, and she told herself she was grateful. She thought—she hoped—she and Morgan were beginning to understand one another, and speculating on what might have happened if he'd attempted to grab her just showed how immature she was. But she couldn't help the unwilling attraction of the image. She was feminine enough to wonder how he really felt about her now.

Beneath the heavy parka, he was wearing a black woollen shirt and a thick sweater. The bulkiness of his clothes helped to disguise his loss of weight, but he still looked so thin she wanted to weep. The feeling came over her totally without warning, and she was glad to have the excuse of hanging away his coat to take her out of the room.

The fridge offered eggs and cheese and the makings of a salad, as well as the remains of the chicken pie she'd made for Graham the night before. She'd intended to have it for her supper, but she couldn't offer that to Morgan. There were potatoes, as well, and some frozen peas in the freezer.

She frowned. She could make a cheese omelette, she mused thoughtfully. She didn't think Morgan would appreciate a salad right now. He needed wholesome food, like eggs and milk and potatoes. Perhaps some chips would be acceptable, and a side-salad to give the meal some colour.

In control of herself again, she went to the living-room door, intending to ask Morgan if he approved of her choice. But to her surprise he'd kicked off his boots and was stretched out on the sofa, and although she couldn't be absolutely sure she thought he was asleep.

Her heart skipped a beat, and, moving cautiously into the room, she approached the sofa on silent feet. He was asleep; he was breathing deeply and his arms were curled above his head, leaving him open to her curious gaze.

He must be exhausted, she thought half guiltily, surprised
at her reaction to his weakness. She'd never known Morgan
to be vulnerable before, and it was a disturbing revelation.
He'd always seemed so confident in the past, and to find
he wasn't invincible after all stirred emotions she preferred
not to identify.

Before going back into the kitchen, she went and got a
rug from upstairs. The food could wait; sleep was obviously
more important to him right now. He didn't stir as she
spread the rug over him, and that surprised her, too. But
she refused to accept that a subconscious awareness of her
presence was the reason he'd found it so easy to relax.

The phone rang about twenty minutes later.

Cursing under her breath, Fliss swung open the kitchen
door and fairly flew across the living room to pick it up.
But the phone was beside the sofa, and Morgan stirred as
she picked up the receiver. Damn, she thought impatiently,
guessing who was calling. She had no wish to have a conversation with Graham with her husband listening in to
every word she said.

'Whittersley 2492,' she said tightly, and then expelled an
unwary breath when her mother-in-law said, 'Felicity? Is
that you?' Who else? thought Fliss, feeling a belated irritation with herself for blaming Graham. If she started getting impatient with him, he'd begin to think she didn't care,
and she did.

'Celia,' she said now, aware of her husband pushing himself up against the cushions behind her. 'Did you want to
speak to Morgan?'

'Morgan!' Celia's exclamation reminded her that her earlier assumption that Morgan had told his parents what he
was doing wasn't true. Stifling a groan, she turned to find
her husband scrubbing the sleep from his eyes and regarding her with a resigned expression. She heard the other
woman catch her breath. 'You mean, he's there!'

'I—well, yes,' Fliss admitted unhappily as Morgan

swung his legs to the floor. She handed the phone to him, silently begging his understanding, and his lips twitched in the ghost of a smile as he raised the handset to his ear.

'Hello, Mum.'

Fliss didn't stay to hear what his mother had to say to him. If she knew Celia, she and James would drive down the following day. So much for the hope that she and Morgan would have a chance to talk to one another over the weekend, she thought ruefully. If her in-laws had seen the article in the *Herald*, they would demand an explanation, too.

Closing the kitchen door, she made a concerted effort to keep busy. She'd already peeled the potatoes and washed the salad, and now she took the eggs out of the fridge. They were locally produced and much bigger than the shop-bought variety, and she was examining them for cracks when Morgan pushed open the door.

'Thanks for nothing,' he said wryly, supporting himself with a hand on either side of the frame.

Her eyes dropped immediately to his feet. He hadn't bothered to put on his boots, and there was something vaguely disturbing about the familiarity that revealed. But she was glad he wasn't angry with her for telling his parents his whereabouts. It was good to be having a civil conversation with him at last.

'I'm sorry,' she said, and meant it. 'But when I heard your mother's voice I'm afraid I instantly assumed they knew where you were.' She grimaced. 'Anyway, what did she ring for? If she didn't know you were here until I told her...'

'You're forgetting about the article in the *Herald*,' he reminded her drily, and Fliss waited anxiously for his mood to change. But it didn't. 'Apparently, they were only waiting for you to get home from work so that they could discuss it with you.' He paused. 'I told them the report was an exaggeration; that you've got no immediate plans to apply for a divorce.'

Fliss breathed a little more freely. 'Thanks.'

'Forget it.' Morgan regarded her consideringly for a few moments, and then gave a shrug. 'That doesn't necessarily mean that I believe it,' he added softly. 'Are you sure you still want me to stay the night?'

'Of course.'

Fliss's response was automatic, but she couldn't deny a fluttering uncertainty in the pit of her stomach at the thought. Was she being entirely wise in encouraging him to stay here? Her previous relationship with Morgan should warn her not to take anything for granted.

'Okay.' Morgan straightened now, rubbing an exploring hand across the stubble on his jaw. 'Well, if you're sure, would you mind if I take a shower? I'm feeling pretty grubby after all that travelling.'

'You can have a bath, if you'd rather,' said Fliss impulsively. 'The bathroom's the first door on the right at the top of the stairs. There are towels in the airing cupboard on the landing.' She paused. 'I'm making omelettes for supper. Is that all right?'

'Whatever.' Morgan didn't sound particularly interested, and she guessed his mind was on other things. 'By the way,' he said ruefully, 'they're coming down in the morning. My parents, I mean. I tried to put them off, but you know what my mother is like.'

Fliss turned towards him. 'That's all right.'

'Is it?'

'Of course.' She shrugged. 'It's not as if they haven't been here before.'

'If you say so.' Morgan sighed. 'As soon as they leave, I'll make other arrangements. I may even go back with them to Tudor Cross, as I said before. Now that they know about your—association with Bland, there doesn't seem much point in continuing this charade.'

It was on the tip of Fliss's tongue to say it wasn't a charade, but she stopped herself. Wasn't this what she wanted, after all? She'd been anxious about telling him about Graham, but now the article had done it for her. Why should she feel any doubt because he wanted to leave?

'That's up to you,' she said now, her voice barely audible as she turned back to the counter. 'Um—by the way, there's plenty of hot water. So don't worry about being economical when you fill the bath.'

Morgan looked as if he would have liked to say something else, but he seemed to think better of it. 'Fine,' he said, somewhat flatly. 'I'll be about fifteen minutes, is that all right?'

'Take as long as you want,' she told him, breaking eggs into a basin. 'It's early yet. I don't usually eat until about six.'

Fliss waited until she'd heard the bathroom door close behind him before venturing into the living room again. Morgan's boots were still lying beside the sofa, where he'd kicked them off, and she picked them up and carried them into the understairs cupboard so that they were out of the way. She saw his parka hanging there, too, and she would have liked to go through his pockets. She doubted she would have found anything interesting, but she was curious to see if he'd kept anything of hers. Like a photograph, for example, or the wallet she'd given him for his birthday. But as they'd destroyed his watch, they'd probably destroyed that, too.

She couldn't help wondering how he'd paid for his train ticket. And it occurred to her suddenly that she owed him at least half the money she'd got when she'd sold the house. Not that it was a lot; they'd still had a hefty mortgage. But she'd saved a little after all expenses were paid.

Sooner or later, she would have to discuss it with him. And the fact that she'd sent most of his clothes to the Red Cross. She'd kept some of his things: his favourite shirt and a couple of his sweaters. She used to wear them for comfort when she was feeling particularly down.

She blew out a trembling breath. She was beginning to feel emotional again, and that wouldn't do. So long as Morgan was here, she had to maintain a sense of detachment—for Graham's sake, if nothing else. But what was Morgan going to do? How was he going to live when he didn't even own his own clothes any more? As she laid the fire and lit it, she was forced to accept that Morgan's return had created problems she hadn't even considered.

CHAPTER SEVEN

THE phone rang again as Fliss was tossing the salad. She'd already peeled and sliced the potatoes and grated some cheese, and the eggs were lightly beaten, waiting to be poured into the pan. She'd also opened a tin of soup, remembering that Morgan preferred savoury things to sweet things, and she had some crumbly granary bread she intended to toast.

This time she had no doubt who was calling. As Morgan's parents had already called, she guessed it was Graham, reporting on what the bishop had said. Thank goodness Morgan was in the bath, she thought, picking up the receiver. But as she gave the number she realised she was speaking in an undertone as if he might overhear.

'There's no need to whisper, Fliss!' Graham exclaimed, ignoring what he'd said that morning. 'I've spoken with the bishop and he was surprisingly understanding about the whole thing. He doesn't like the publicity, of course, but apart from that he was quite sympathetic. And I've assured him that nothing like that will happen again.'

'Have you?'

Fliss knew her response was rather tart, and, sensitive to her every mood, Graham evidently thought he'd been a little too self-congratulatory. 'As I said last night, that doesn't mean we can't see one another, my dear. You know my feelings, and I wish it could be different. And it will be, once this—this little contretemps is over.'

Fliss could imagine how Morgan would react to being called a 'little contretemps', but she couldn't blame Graham because she was feeling edgy now. 'I know,' she said, and then, because she couldn't let him find out from one of her neighbours, 'By the way, um—Morgan's here.'

There was complete silence for several seconds and she guessed her confession had robbed him of speech. After all, the last thing either of them had expected was that her husband should just turn up on her doorstep. Although, now she came to think of it, it was exactly the sort of thing she should have expected Morgan to do.

'I didn't know he was coming,' she added quickly, just in case he thought differently. 'He—er—he'd read the article, too.'

'I see.' Graham sounded apprehensive now. 'And was he very angry? I mean, how did he take it?' He caught his breath. 'Oh, no. Don't answer that. I expect he's listening in to this call.'

Fliss sighed. 'He's not listening,' she assured him drily, wondering what he expected Morgan to do. If she didn't know how ridiculous it was, she'd have said Graham was nervous. For heaven's sake, surely he wasn't afraid that Morgan might accuse him of seducing his wife?

'Anyway, what do you mean?' he asked, after a moment's consideration. 'When you say he's there, is he having supper with you, or what?'

Or what, thought Fliss drily, but she didn't say it. 'He—well, I've offered him a bed for the night. It was much too late when he arrived to get back to Craythorpe this evening, and his parents are coming to see him tomorrow morning.'

'You mean, he's staying with you? At the cottage?' For all his misgivings, she could fairly feel the disapproval in his voice. 'I can't believe you've asked him to stay with you, Fliss. For heaven's sake, you said he was like a stranger. Am I allowed to ask where he intends to sleep?'

'In the spare room, of course.' Fliss was hurt that he should feel the need to ask that question in the circumstances. She straightened her spine. 'I'd better go. I'm in the middle of preparing the meal.'

'Oh, Fliss!' Graham sounded ashamed of himself now. 'Please don't be angry with me because I'm jealous. It's just so hard to accept that you still have a relationship with this man.'

Fliss sighed. 'We don't have a relationship, Graham. But he's still my husband and I can't just turn him out.'

'Of course, of course.' Graham attempted to rebuild his fences. 'I just wish I had the freedom to be there with you.'

'Do you?'

Fliss could have said that when he'd had the chance to stay he hadn't taken it. But that would have been unkind, and she had to respect his beliefs. Graham was Graham, and nothing she could do would change him. She shouldn't blame him for being faithful to his vows.

'Well, I suppose I'd better let you go and attend to your visitor,' he remarked ruefully. 'Um—if he's not in the room with you now, where has he gone?'

'He's having a bath,' said Fliss tersely, wondering if his reasons for asking were objective or personal. 'I trust you don't have any objections to that?'

'Don't be silly.' But there was relief in his voice for all that. He sighed. 'I don't suppose I'll see you tomorrow, then.'

'Oh—the bring-and-buy sale,' said Fliss, realising she'd forgotten all about it. Was it just her or wasn't he a little insensitive to bring it up? 'No, I'm afraid not.'

'Well, never mind.' Graham weathered his disappointment manfully. 'Perhaps you could give me a ring tomorrow night instead?'

'All right.'

Fliss agreed, but after she'd rung off she spent some moments staring at the phone. For tomorrow night read 'after Morgan leaves', she brooded frustratedly. Was Graham aware what an unsatisfactory call that had been?

A board creaking upstairs distracted her. Tilting her head towards the ceiling, she wondered if it was Morgan getting

out of the bath. But the sound wasn't repeated, and it occurred to her that he'd been much longer than the fifteen
minutes he'd promised. Was he all right? Had he fallen
asleep? Ought she to go up and find out?

Going to the foot of the stairs, she called, 'Morgan?'
rather tentatively.

There was no reply and she bit her lip before placing
one foot on the bottom stair. She didn't want to startle him,
but if he was asleep she'd have to disturb him. He might
have been enjoying the experience, but the water must be
cold by now.

She paused outside the bathroom door and put her ear to
the panels. But the door was thick and all she could hear
was the sound of water trickling into the cistern nearby.
'Morgan,' she said again, gripping the handle. 'Um—it's
getting on for six. Shall I start the meal?'

'Why not?'

Fliss gasped. She couldn't help it. The voice had come
from the opposite side of the landing. Turning, she found
Morgan leaning against the doorway of her bedroom, his
shirt hanging open over his bare chest and the button at the
waistband of his black trousers unfastened, too.

'What—where were—?'

'I was looking for a razor,' he said without apology,
rubbing a rueful hand over the gold-tipped stubble deco-
rating his chin. 'I would have asked you first, but I could
hear you talking to somebody, so I thought you wouldn't
mind if I looked for myself.'

Fliss did mind. She minded a lot. She didn't like the idea
of Morgan riffling through her belongings, searching the
drawers in the dressing table, finding mementoes she'd hidden away. This was her home, not his, and he had no right
to take advantage of it. But what she minded most was the
warmth that spread through her as she looked at him.

Her eyes were drawn against her will to his lean brown
torso, where a triangle of sun-bleached hair arrowed down

to his waist. Muscle, ribbed and hard, flexed taut across the hollow of his stomach, and a scar she'd never seen before was a jagged white line against his brown flesh.

Her own stomach hollowed, and she tore her eyes away from the glimpse of underwear visible in the opened vee of his trousers. But that didn't stop her being aware of it, or prevent an instinctive quickening between her legs.

Oh, God!

'Graham phoned,' she informed him tersely, wondering what he might have overheard. 'And—and the only razor I have is in the bathroom cabinet.' She pressed her palms together. 'What did you expect to find?'

Morgan shrugged, apparently not at all put out by her obvious pique. If he was aware of how frustrated she felt, he didn't show it, and Fliss thought how stupid she was to let him affect her in this way.

For heaven's sake, she chided herself crossly, his half naked body should hardly be a novelty to her. But it was; she'd forgotten how physical their relationship had been. Despite all her efforts to ignore him, her body was responding to the sensual memories his evoked.

'I told you, I was looking for a razor,' Morgan replied evenly. 'I wasn't rummaging through your knicker drawer, if that's what you're implying.'

'I never said—' Fliss broke off, halting in some confusion. She could hardly accuse him of looking for proof that Graham had shared her bed. She squared her shoulders. 'It doesn't matter,' she added. 'And I only have the electric razor you've probably seen. I can go down to the stores if you like and get you another.'

'Don't you think that might arouse some curiosity?' he enquired drily. 'Or are you in the habit of buying razors for men?' He saw her indignation and shook his head half mockingly. 'No. I'll wait until the morning. It's not as if we'll be sleeping together, is it?'

Fliss's face burned. 'No,' she replied stiffly, sure now

that he had heard her conversation with Graham. Or her half of it, anyway, she amended, trying to remember everything she'd said. She recalled Graham's demand to know where her husband was sleeping. Was her reference to the spare bedroom responsible for this?

'Okay.' Was it her imagination, or was there a silent threat in those cool grey eyes? 'I'll finish dressing,' he added, crossing the landing to enter the bathroom. 'I shan't be long,' he remarked carelessly, and closed the door in her face.

Fliss breathed deeply, trying to calm herself. Dammit, he had no right to behave as if she had something to hide. She'd done nothing wrong, but she doubted he'd ever believe her. Why couldn't he accept that it wasn't her fault that she'd thought he was dead?

Or his...

Pushing back an errant strand that had come loose from her braid behind her ear, she stepped almost irresistibly into the doorway of her bedroom. She looked intently about her, but she could see no evidence that he had been prying into her things. The room looked essentially feminine, she thought, with its swagged dressing table and matching flower-printed curtains at the windows. Even the bedspread was pink satin. She'd bought it to replace the cream damask that had been a wedding present to her and Morgan.

Deciding she was allowing his presence to spook her, she closed the door behind her and went downstairs. As Morgan was almost ready, she could start the supper. With a bit of luck, there'd be no more calls tonight.

Morgan appeared as she was laying the small table in the living room. The cottage had only two rooms downstairs and when she was on her own she usually ate in the kitchen. There was an Aga in there that kept the kitchen warm and cosy, but she wanted to avoid that kind of intimacy tonight.

'Can I do anything?' he asked, surveying the white cloth

and the mosaic-patterned place-mats with interest. 'Hey—'
his lips tilted '—didn't we get these mats as a wedding
present, too?'

'Too?'

Fliss looked at him suspiciously and he grimaced. 'As
well as the bedside lamps you've got upstairs.'

'I bought the mats,' replied Fliss flatly, carrying the tu-
reen of soup through from the kitchen and setting it in the
middle of the table. 'The ones Doug and Cheryl Lewis
bought us are put away.'

Morgan frowned. 'Doug and Cheryl Lewis,' he repeated
softly. 'I wonder how they're getting on these days?'

'They're divorced,' said Fliss, aware that her tone was
slightly bitter. 'About a year ago, Doug decided to trade
Cheryl in for a younger model.'

Morgan stared at her blankly. 'You're kidding.'

'No, I'm not.' Fliss put the bread basket on the table and
indicated that he should sit down. 'I guess half our
friends—or rather half *your* friends,' she corrected herself
drily, remembering that most of the couples they'd been
friendly with in London had drifted away after Morgan had
disappeared, 'are divorced now. Those that actually got
married, of course. These days, living together is far more
convenient. You can just walk out when you feel like it.'

'Is that what you believe?' asked Morgan coolly, leaving
her with a feeling of ambivalence. She believed in marriage—but did she want to say that to him?

'Why don't you have a roll?' she asked, avoiding an
answer, and, picking up a bowl, she ladled some of the
soup into it.

'It's chicken,' she said, feeling the need to keep the conversation going. 'And I've fried some potatoes, to have
with the omelettes.'

Morgan tasted the soup, but she could tell from his expression that he wasn't enthusiastic. 'And if it's all the same
to you I'll pass on the potatoes,' he said, laying down his

spoon. He broke a piece of bread, but she noticed he didn't put any butter on it. 'I haven't got much of an appetite these days. I'm sorry. I should have warned you, I'm only used to eating once a day.'

Fliss stared at him. 'Only once a day?' she echoed, mentally kicking herself for not considering how he'd lost so much weight.

'Well, we had bananas, sometimes, and I acquired quite a taste for green oranges,' he added. 'They don't look so good—the oranges, I mean. But they're very sweet.'

She shook her head. 'But why didn't you have proper food?' she protested.

Morgan propped his chin on the knuckles of one hand and gave her a resigned look. 'Guess,' he said flatly as she felt her colour rising. 'I was a prisoner, Fliss. I know you don't believe me, but no one was going to do me any favours.'

'Even so...'

'Even so, nobody was getting enough to eat, as it happens. A rebel army has to forage for food where it can. There aren't too many supermarkets in the jungle. Sometimes we existed on a kind of mulched grain for weeks on end.'

He took another mouthful of soup but Fliss found her own appetite had disappeared. It had been easier to deal with the situation when she'd been able to convince herself that Morgan had had it easy. His apparent friendship with Julius Mdola had blinded her to the real ordeal he'd faced every day.

'This is good,' he said, but he laid down his spoon again and she had the feeling he was just being polite. It reminded her, too, of the time he'd spent in the hospital in Kantanga, and her insensitivity to his physical state appalled her now.

She managed to swallow a few more mouthfuls of soup but when it became evident that Morgan was only toying with his food she got up and cleared the bowls away. The omelettes looked so uninviting now that she'd had time to reconsider. A poached egg on toast would have probably been more acceptable, and she wondered if he thought she was as unfeeling as she did herself.

'I'm sorry if you've gone to a lot of unnecessary trouble on my behalf.'

He had come to the door of the kitchen and now stood regarding her with vaguely sympathetic eyes. But there was a tightness about his mouth that hinted at other emotions, and she wished she'd had some warning of his arrival.

'It doesn't matter,' she said, glad that she'd put the fried potatoes in the oven to keep warm. 'Er—perhaps you should tell me what you'd like. I—I haven't had much experience in a situation like this.'

'Nor me,' he conceded wryly, though she had the distinct impression he wasn't talking about the meal. 'If it's all the same to you, I'd prefer a glass of milk. I guess my stomach isn't used to so much food.'

'No problem.' Fliss took a carton of milk from the fridge and poured some into a glass. 'Shall we go back into the other room?'

Morgan frowned. 'What about your supper?'

'I'll get it later,' she replied quickly. She poured herself a cup of coffee from the pot she'd made earlier. 'This will do for now.'

She waited until he was ensconced on the sofa again before seating herself in the armchair opposite, as before. The fact that the fire was lit now made the situation that much brighter, but the atmosphere between them was still cool. Not that that stopped her being aware of him. She was acutely conscious of his lean frame reclining on her sofa. More so now, since she'd seen him semi-naked, and her lips were dry as she searched anxiously for something to say.

'What—what did you do?' she asked at last, and at his

look of enquiry she added, 'All day, I mean. Where did you stay?'

'At a place called Jamara,' he answered evenly. 'You won't have heard of it. It's way up in the mountains, miles from any kind of civilisation. It's where Mdola had his headquarters. We lived in a kind of fortified compound. It was an easy place to defend.'

Fliss licked her lips. 'Did you try to escape?'

Morgan regarded her with weary eyes. 'I'm not a hero, Fliss. I'm just a man who made staying alive his priority.'

Fliss bent her head. 'It wasn't a criticism,' she said defensively. 'But you've told me very little about how you lived. Four years is a long time. What did you do to pass the time?'

Morgan shrugged. 'I wrote.'

'You wrote!' Fliss stared at him now. 'What did you write?'

'This and that.' Morgan emptied his glass and swiped the smear of milk from his top lip with the back of his hand. 'I guess I kept a record of my experiences. I thought I might be able to use it if—when—I got out.'

Fliss absorbed this, and as if he was able to deduce what she was thinking Morgan's mouth took on a sardonic twist. 'It was a piece of cake,' he said. 'A four year sabbatical in the jungle. Nothing to do but write to my heart's content.'

Fliss regarded him warily. 'You have to admit, it does sound unusual.'

'And it was,' he agreed, leaning forward and resting his forearms on his thighs. 'Fliss, I had to do something or I'd have gone mad. Julius knew this, and he let me use an old machine they'd found when they sacked a schoolhouse.'

Fliss frowned. 'What kind of a machine?'

'Well, it wasn't a computer,' he replied drily. 'It was a Remington that must have been at least fifty years old. Julius had been using it to type the propaganda notices they smuggled into Kantanga, and he agreed to let me use it if I'd type the notices, too.'

Fliss shook her head. 'It sounds—it sounds—'

'Idyllic?' he suggested cynically, but she shook her head.

'Incredible,' she amended. 'And this man was your friend?'

'We became friends,' Morgan corrected her quietly. 'Look—we were at university together, but we weren't friends. We recognised each other when we met, but until I arrived at Jamara I don't think either one of us knew who we were dealing with. Or I didn't certainly. Julius may have recognised my name. In any event, I was brought there for a purpose, and I was never allowed to forget it.'

'But, didn't you ask him if he'd known it was you?'

'No.' Morgan sighed. 'I hardly saw him. And when I did we had more important matters to deal with. Like, if he didn't overthrow Ungave, we'd none of us make it out of there alive.'

Fliss felt a quiver of fear attack her stomach. For a moment, she felt physically sick. It was so easy to forget he'd been in danger. That he'd been living with an army that was virtually under siege.

'Anyway, that's enough about that,' he said flatly. 'I am alive, and I guess we have to deal with it. But until I find out what my financial obligations are I guess I have no choice but to stay with Mum and Dad.'

Fliss sucked in a breath. 'You could stay here.'

The invitation had been instinctive then—drawn as much from the guilt she felt at having sold the house in Chaucer Road, she assured herself, as by any real desire to prolong their association. But as soon as it was issued she felt another kind of culpability: to Graham, and the promises they'd exchanged.

'Could I?'

Morgan's response was so swift, she wondered if he'd planned it all along. 'Of course,' she said stiffly, getting up

to draw the curtains. She switched on the standard lamp.
'It's my fault that you don't have a home.'

'So it is.' He was sardonic, and she saw him watching
her with narrowed eyes. 'Well, can we talk about this tomorrow? Right now, I'm bushed, if you'll forgive the pun.
I'd like to go to bed.'

For a heart-stopping moment, she thought he meant
something more than his words had stated, and a trickle of
unwilling excitement slid down her spine. Oh, God, she
thought, I don't know if I can handle this. How would she
react if he chose to demand his rights?

But when he got to his feet, and her eyes widened in
unknowing anticipation, nothing happened. 'The spare
room, I think you said,' he remarked, flexing his back. And
it wasn't until he'd left her staring after him that she remembered she'd said nothing of the sort to him…

CHAPTER EIGHT

MORGAN slept badly, despite the fact that the bed was comfortable and there were no external noises to disturb him.

Or perhaps because of those things, he reflected, staring at the ceiling as the first rays of a watery sun forced their way through a crack in the curtains. He wasn't used to the unearthly quiet of an English country village.

And he was tired; still. He had been deathly tired when he came to bed, but the fitful sleep he'd had had only taken the edge off his exhaustion. Now, he felt weary, with a desperate need to escape the bitterness of his thoughts.

He sighed, rolling onto his side and punching his pillow with a balled fist. The trouble was, he couldn't forget that Fliss was sleeping in the room next door, that very feminine room, with its flowered curtains and pink satin bedspread. He hadn't been able to resist going in there the night before, and although he hadn't exactly been lying when he'd said he was looking for a razor it had only been an excuse.

He'd wanted to catch her out. He'd wanted to find something of Bland's, to prove to himself, as well as to her, that she had been lying, too. He couldn't believe that any man who was as close to Fliss as this man evidently was could resist getting into her bed. Dammit, they'd only known one another a matter of hours before he'd known a burning desire to make love to her, and it seemed inconceivable that Bland should have passed up such an opportunity.

He hadn't found anything, of course, but that didn't mean that nothing had happened. They'd been *engaged*, for God's sake. What proof did he need? A drawer full of condoms, or Bland's slippers tucked confidingly beneath the bed?

Morgan frowned, flinging himself onto his back again as the anguish his thoughts were causing brought a physical ache to his gut. It didn't help to tell himself that he'd been afraid of just such a situation. The abstract images he'd entertained when he was imprisoned at Jamara bore no resemblance to what was actually happening now. Even the frustration he'd suffered at Craythorpe seemed puny by comparison. She was his wife, wasn't she? She was still his wife, and he'd be damned if he'd give her up without a fight.

He rolled onto his stomach and reached for the clock that resided on the bedside table. It was a quarter to six, he saw broodingly. What the hell time did Fliss usually get up? He was used to rising early, earlier still if you took West African time into consideration, and although he still felt tired it wasn't something he could cure right now.

Pushing back the duvet, he swung his feet to the floor. Although the sun was shining outside, it was cold in the bedroom, and he scowled at his reflection in the wardrobe mirror at the foot of the bed. He had to remember goosebumps were an occupational hazard when you chose to sleep without pyjamas. The suitcase he'd taken to Nyanda had been consumed in the blaze they'd made of his transport, and as Fliss had assumed he was dead it was unlikely that she'd have hung onto the shorts and tee shirts he'd occasionally been known to wear.

Hunching his shoulders, he got to his feet, and shuffled over to the windows. He grabbed his sweater in passing, and yanked it over his head. His jaw was rough; he really would have to try and buy a razor before his mother saw him, he reflected ruefully. She'd been horrified at his appearance at Craythorpe, but his hand had got slightly steadier since then.

Well, slightly, he conceded, peering through the curtains. Since he'd arrived at the cottage, his nerves had suffered something of a reverse. He took a breath. There was no one waiting at the gate or watching the house, he saw, his toes curling appreciatively against the soft carpet. It felt good; he'd got used to the chill of packed earth beneath his bare feet.

There was a radiator beneath the window, but it was cold, and he guessed it was timed to come on nearer to seven o'clock. If he went downstairs, he could always light a fire, he thought consideringly. Surely Fliss wouldn't object if he didn't make any noise.

It was colder still on the landing. The only heat here was what drifted out of the bedrooms or up the stairs. It wasn't big enough to warrant its own radiator. Just the bathroom door, the spare-room door—and the door into Fliss's room.

The temptation was irresistible. Knowing she must still be asleep made the decision inevitable, and, gripping the handle of the door, he firmly turned it.

As in the room he'd occupied, the sun was already shifting the shadows, making it easy for him to see the bed. The pink satin coverlet had been folded back and Fliss was hidden beneath the hump of bedding. No duvets here, he noticed. Just good old-fashioned blankets and sheets.

He knew he shouldn't go any further. Fliss was asleep, and he had no right to enter her room uninvited. And then he thought of Graham Bland, and his good intentions hardened. Stepping over the threshold, he let the door swing to behind him, and walked lightly across to the bed.

Fliss was lying on her side, her lashes like dark fans against the curve of her cheeks. Her hair was loose on the pillow, and her lips were slightly parted, the warmth of her breathing fanning his bare knee as he stood looking down at her. Then, unable to stop himself, he squatted down beside her and stroked her cheek with trembling fingers.

It was so soft. He caught his breath as the calluses on his hands brushed her skin. He'd forgotten how soft her skin was, how sweet she smelled. As she stirred, he caught her fragrance, and he felt dizzy for a moment.

When she opened her eyes, he was unprepared for it. She'd seemed so deeply asleep that he hadn't suspected his light touch might cause her to wake. But she was looking at him now, though he had the strangest feeling she wasn't seeing him. If she was, she wouldn't be smiling, whereas there was a definite tilt to her soft lips.

'Morgan...'

She said his name barely audibly, and as he'd come in here prepared to confront her anger he was pleasantly surprised by her response.

'Hi,' he answered, resisting the urge to tuck an ebony strand of hair behind her ear. 'Did I wake you?'

Fliss blinked, as if she couldn't quite believe her eyes, and then slowly shook her head. 'It doesn't matter,' she said, her tongue appearing to moisten her upper lip. 'Are you cold?' she added. 'You've got a sweater on.'

'I'm okay,' he assured her, hearing the involuntary thickening in his voice. 'I was going to go downstairs and light the fire, and it's too cold to hang around in just my shorts.'

'Your shorts?' There was a question in her words now, and she pushed the covers aside to stare at his bony knees. 'Oh, yes,' she said, with a catch in her voice. 'You must have been cold. You don't usually wear anything to sleep in.'

Now it was Morgan's turn to catch his breath. Apart from the unknowing provocation of her words, she had also exposed the creamy slopes of her breasts. She was wearing a satin nightgown, but there were inserts of lace across the bodice, and although her nipples were covered the dusky areolas were plain to see.

His reaction staggered him. He'd thought that sex might prove a problem, but the discomfort between his legs proved that wasn't so. Or, at least, he was having a normal erection. Whether or not he could sustain it was something he was unlikely to find out.

He swallowed convulsively.

In those early days at Jamara, he'd been too weak to think about sex, or to wonder what its absence might do to him. He'd been glad to be alive, to have a roof over his head and a room of his own, and so long as they hadn't bothered him he hadn't cared how his fellow internees handled their own abstinence. Later, when he was stronger and Mdola had allowed him the run of the camp again, he'd seen women occasionally, but he'd never been tempted to invite any of them into his quarters. Even though there'd been times when he could have done. A functional mating had had no appeal, apart from anything else. He'd had dreams, of course. But that was different. A living, breathing woman hadn't been involved.

Not like this.

Not like Fliss.

Fliss was stretching now, putting her arms above her head, reaching for the iron rails that formed the head of the bed. She was rosily pink, soft and warm and feminine. He wanted to slide his hands beneath her and haul her into his arms.

She caught him watching her, but instead of resenting it she cast him a sensuous look. Oh, God, he thought, she was so beautiful. Did she have any idea what she was doing to him?

Of course she did.

Impatient with himself for even doubting it, he drew a steadying breath and wondered what she expected him to do. The night before, she'd been so careful to keep her distance. But, suddenly, he didn't know what she was thinking any more.

'Fliss...'

Her name slipped softly from his lips, and her dark brows formed an arch above eyes that were a delicate shade of violet. Was he only imagining the invitation in them? he wondered. Was she not yet quite awake? Was he mistaking a sleepy lethargy for sensuality?

'Fliss,' he said again, more hoarsely now, giving in to
the impulse to run unsteady fingers along her bare arm to
her shoulder. 'God, you have no idea how I've missed you,'
he added, though the words were barely audible, even to
him. 'Sometimes, I used to wish I was dead.'

He expected her to stop him. He expected her to push
him away and order him out of her bedroom. After all,
she'd more or less made it clear that they didn't have a
relationship any longer. They hadn't really discussed it, but
he had sensed that, however she phrased it, she hadn't
given Bland up.

But she didn't do any of those things. Even when he
combed his fingers through her hair before trailing them
sensuously down her throat, she simply lay there watching
him. His own heart might be beating wildly, but she seemed
to be in complete control of her emotions. Perhaps she
wasn't so different from the night before after all. Perhaps
she was just waiting to see how far he intended to go.

His breathing grew ragged. His knees were aching and
an attack of pins and needles was causing a burning sensation in his hip. Dammit, he thought, he was kidding himself by thinking he was strong enough to handle this. Apart
from being physically malnourished, emotionally he was
starved, and she was doing nothing to assuage his hunger.

Unable to stand the pain any longer, he dragged himself
to his feet and stood looking down at her through narrowed
eyes. 'I might as well go and light that fire,' he said curtly,
hoping his legs would support him, but when he would
have turned away she came up on her elbows and caught
his hand.

'I'm sorry,' she said, but instead of appeasing his anger
her words only infuriated him even more. What did she
think he was made of, for God's sake? Stone? Didn't she
know that even ordinary prisoners were horny after a spell
in jail?

'Are you?' he asked, feeling his instantaneous response

to the provocation she represented with a bitter sense of irony. 'How sorry?'

Her hand fell away, and her eyes mirrored the confusion she was feeling. 'I don't know what you—what you—'

'Mean?' he asked harshly as the strength in his legs returned, and she shook her head.

'No.' She licked her lips, and he guessed she had no idea how much he wanted to do that for her. 'I meant—I don't know what you—want from me.'

'Oh, come on!' Morgan made a derisive sound. 'You'll be telling me next that you've forgotten how to do it. What do you think I want? Sympathy?'

Fliss's lips parted, and as if just realising how provoking her appearance was she clutched a handful of the sheet and pressed it to her throat.

Morgan was suddenly furious. His own weaknesses were hard enough to deal with without having her behave as if she had something to hide. He'd seen her naked, for God's sake. He'd undressed her himself more times than he could remember, and he'd be damned if he'd let her treat him like some kind of pitiful voyeur.

Without stopping to think what he was doing, without considering the consequences of his actions at all, he bent and stripped the covers from her, tossing them carelessly over the rail at the foot of the bed. Then, before she could scramble across the bed and escape him, he came down beside her, pinning her in place with one hand at either side of her struggling form.

'What do you think I want?' he said again, staring down at her with eyes that were almost opaque with desire. His voice thickened. 'I want you, Fliss. I want you. I've thought of nothing else since I got back.'

'No—'

Her shocked denial was cut off by the grim determination of his mouth. Her struggles were easily overwhelmed by the weight of his lean body, and he threw one leg across her thighs to keep her where she was. With one hand entwined in her hair and the other curled possessively about her nape, Morgan took his time exploring her lips. He was hungry for her, that was true, but he tried to leash his passion, even though his tongue did force its way between her teeth.

It was heaven and it was hell, he thought unsteadily, though there was little room for either in his inflamed mind. His senses were spinning with the realisation that this was Fliss's lissome body he could feel beneath him, and his hand slid from her neck to frame the generous contours of her breast.

Her heart was palpitating now. He could feel it. Its erratic beat pulsed in concert with his own. When he caressed her breast, she quivered, as if she was losing control of her body, and her nipple pushed urgently against his palm.

And then she stopped struggling. She seemed to realise that, whatever she did, her own needs were bound to betray her, and the fist that had been balled against his middle was suddenly clutching the wool of his sweater and pulling him closer. Her lips parted, and he had the crazy sensation that he was in danger of drowning in her sweetness, and then her other hand burrowed beneath the hem of his sweater and insinuated itself into the waistband of his shorts.

His reaction was painful. God! A shudder ran over his skin, but he wasn't cold. On the contrary, he felt as if he was burning up with fever and only Fliss had the cure. The hand that searched and found the hem of her nightgown was fairly trembling with anticipation, and for a fleeting moment he wondered how long he could sustain such a high level of emotional intensity.

Fliss was responding to him now. Her mouth had softened, and she was making little sounds of pleasure as he continued to explore her lips. The sounds she uttered made him crazy, and he wondered if she had any idea how provocative they were. Added to the sensuous brush of her fingers across his bare hip, they were driving him to distraction.

With a groan, he felt the smoothness of her thigh beneath the satin nightgown, and the way her legs jerked when he put his hand between her knees. If he hadn't known better, he'd have thought she'd never done anything like this before, and he had a brief image of how he'd taken her virginity all those years ago.

But this was different, he acknowledged. For one thing, they were different people, and although he didn't want to think about it now he couldn't forget he was doing this against her will. The response he was arousing in her was an instinctive thing, not an emotional need. When it was over, she'd come to her senses and hate him for what he'd done.

But what the hell? he argued with himself. She was still his wife. No one with an ounce of humanity would blame him for taking advantage of it. And, God damn it, she wanted him, whether she was aware of it or not. Her yielding form fairly shouted surrender, and he was only human, after all.

His hand slid gently upwards. It met no resistance, though the muscles in her thighs quivered a little as he reached the cleft between her legs. She was wet, he realised as his fingers probed the damp curls and found her. She seemed unable to prevent herself from arching against that invasion, and he guessed he had only to caress her to send her over the edge.

He shuddered again, only this time it was not with anticipation. Panic, pure and simple, was what filmed his skin with moisture and cooled his blood. He couldn't do it, he thought sickly. He couldn't give her what she wanted. His arousal shrank pitifully as he tore himself away.

There was a moment of complete humiliation, when he sat on the side of the bed, with his head in his hands, and waited for the words of contempt that he was sure were to follow. Oh, God, he thought bitterly, was that what he'd become? An impotent manifestation of the man he used to be?

'Morgan?'

There didn't seem to be any censure in her voice, but Morgan wasn't prepared to stick around until there was. 'I'll go and make some tea,' he said, getting abruptly to his feet. 'I guess we could both use some.'

'Wait!' Flushing as she pushed her nightgown over her knees again, Fliss swung her legs over the side of the bed. 'I—what is it, Morgan?' she demanded anxiously. 'I thought—' She took a breath. 'Did I do something wrong?'

Morgan hesitated. He could have told her what had happened. He could have admitted that it wasn't her, it was him; that he'd been afraid he'd let her down. His years of exile had taken a toll on him that he was only now beginning to understand. He'd chickened out of making a bigger fool of himself by calling a halt.

But he didn't do that. Instead, he hid his shame behind a mask of anger. 'I decided I didn't want to sleep with Bland's mistress, after all,' he declared cruelly, and, without waiting for her response, he left the room.

CHAPTER NINE

FLISS stood at the kitchen window staring out at the daffodils that were struggling to survive in the small garden outside. For the past few days, the wind and rain had played havoc with all the plants, and the yellow heads were drooping pathetically.

They looked like she felt, she reflected dismally, wondering what her husband was doing today. She doubted he was thinking about her, but that didn't stop her from worrying about him. It was almost a week since he'd returned to Craythorpe and she'd had no word from him since then.

She wished she could ring his parents and ask them if they'd heard from him, but if she did that they'd be bound to ask why she didn't ring the base herself. As far as they were concerned, she and Morgan still cared about one another. Despite their dismay at reading about her relationship with Graham in the newspaper, Morgan had managed to convince them it was all an exaggeration.

And she'd been grateful that he'd said that last weekend. After the way he'd treated her, after that abortive assault on her emotions in the bedroom, she'd been in no state to cope with his mother's recriminations, and she'd been half afraid he was going to expose his disgust to them.

But he hadn't. Instead, he'd let her off the hook and taken it upon himself to explain. She'd still been trying to understand what had happened when the Rikers arrived, and she'd had little time to come to terms with the situation before they put her on the spot.

In fact, she still didn't actually know what had happened, or indeed why. During the past week, she'd had plenty of time to try to come up with an explanation, but all she'd

done was compound her own guilt. Whatever explanation Morgan had given his parents, she'd known that it
wasn't the truth. Apart from anything else, he'd made it
brutally plain what he thought of her, and every time she
thought of the way she'd behaved she wanted to bury her
head in the sand.

She had no excuses for herself. When she'd awakened
that morning and found Morgan beside her bed she could
easily have turned him away. All right, perhaps she had
been a little confused to begin with, but she'd known exactly what she was doing when she'd caught his hand.

She shuddered. Of course, she'd had no idea how violently he might react to her. Even knowing he'd been in-
carcerated in a jungle prison for four years, she had not
been prepared for what came next. She was used to
Graham, who would never have treated her in such a way.
Which was another reason why she hated herself now. Had
she really forgotten all they meant to one another in the
heated passion of Morgan's embrace?

Heated?

Passion?

Fliss's lips quivered now as she remembered how bitterly
disappointed she had been. What Morgan had done had
been equally—no, *more*—unforgivable. However much she
might blame herself for initiating it, nothing could alter the
fact that he'd deliberately used sex as a weapon to punish
her.

She shuddered again, turning from the window as the
memories she'd tried hard to avoid returned to taunt her.
God, how he must have been laughing at her, she tormented
herself painfully. She'd been so weak, so eager, so *easy*!
She'd invited him to take advantage of her, and he had.

His only saving grace was that he hadn't gloated about
his victory. But perhaps the fact that she'd made sure she
was in the bathroom, with the door safely locked, when he
returned with the tea had balked his plan. In any event,

when he'd tapped at the bathroom door to tell her that he'd left a mug of tea beside her bed she'd pretended not to hear him, and to her relief he hadn't spoken to her again until she went downstairs.

She remembered she'd dressed at high speed, half afraid he might change his mind and come back, but she needn't have worried. When she'd eventually ventured down the stairs, he'd already got the fire going in the living room, and there was the heavenly scent of brewing coffee drifting out of the kitchen. However quick she'd been, evidently he had been quicker, though the growth of beard on his chin showed that he hadn't yet been able to shave.

Breakfast—Fliss had only wanted coffee—had been a tense meal, but to her relief Morgan hadn't mentioned what had happened upstairs. On the contrary, he'd seemed as eager as she was to ignore it, and although there'd been no real conversation as such they had managed to get through the next couple of hours without further recriminations.

The Rikers had arrived at a quarter to ten. Fliss was in the kitchen, trying to find jobs to distract herself, when she heard their familiar rat-a-tat at the door. There were reporters at the gate again, but she'd guessed Celia and James would ignore them. After the distress the photograph of Fliss and Graham had caused, Morgan's parents were unlikely to do or say anything to encourage the media's curiosity.

She'd heard Morgan go to answer the door, and she'd known she ought to be with him. Unless she wanted the Rikers to think the worst, she had to behave as if everything was normal. She couldn't be sure of what Morgan was going to say, of course, but she'd hoped he wouldn't let her down.

One of the hardest things she had ever done was to go into the living room to greet the visitors. It didn't matter that Morgan had ostensibly explained the circumstances of her relationship with Graham; she'd still felt as if she had

betrayed their trust. And there was no doubt that her
mother-in-law's eyes had initially been cool and calculating. Celia didn't forgive easily, and Morgan was her only
offspring.

'Felicity.' She greeted her daughter-in-law politely, with
none of the warmth and spontaneity she had usually shown.
'So you're still together.' She glanced at Morgan. 'I'm surprised. I half expected you'd be at one another's throats by
now.'

'Cee!' Before his son could respond, her husband gave
her a warning look. Bending to kiss Fliss's flushed cheek,
he patted her shoulder reassuringly. 'Take no notice, my
dear. We both understand how lonely you must have been.'

Fliss managed a tense smile, but she was aware of
Morgan watching her through narrowed lids. He looked so
sombre suddenly, she wondered if he suspected his father's
relationship with her, too. But then his expression cleared,
and he invited his mother to sit down. 'There is such a
thing as poetic licence,' he remarked drily. 'It wouldn't
have been half such a good story without a little exaggeration.'

Celia seated herself on the sofa, but she didn't look convinced. 'You mean, you weren't engaged to this man,
Felicity?' she enquired tartly. 'I must say, if you were, you
never said a word to us.'

Fliss licked her lips. 'Well—' she began uncertainly, not
quite knowing how to continue, and once again Morgan
took a hand.

'They were close friends,' he said. 'He offered—spiritual
support when she most needed it. Fliss is a beautiful
woman. You can't blame the guy if he got the wrong impression.'

Fliss swallowed. Meeting her husband's eyes just then,
she was fairly sure that he didn't believe his own words.
And that reference to 'spiritual support' was his way of

reminding her of his scepticism. But there was no way she could tell them the truth.

'Well, I can't deny I'm relieved.' Evidently his mother was prepared to take his words at face value. 'I've met the man, of course. Felicity introduced us some time ago. But he's hardly the type to attract a woman like her.'

'Why not?'

For a moment, Fliss thought she had asked that question. It so closely mirrored her thoughts at that moment. But it was Morgan who had voiced his own curiosity at his mother's words.

'Well...' Ignoring her husband's disapproval, Celia carefully crossed her slender legs. 'He's so—so fat and—boring, darling. He's not at all like you.'

'He's not fat.' Fliss couldn't allow her to get away with that. 'He's a little overweight, but that's not his fault. His housekeeper will insist on serving him suet puddings!'

'Then he should refuse to eat them,' declared Celia, not at all ashamed of what she'd said. Her lips twitched. 'Oh, Felicity, don't pretend you don't agree with me. I notice you don't deny that he's boring, as well.'

'He's not boring.' Fliss wished she had the nerve to tell them she loved him and not their precious son. 'He's—helped me a lot, and I'm—very fond of him. I don't care what you think of him. He's been very kind to me.'

'I'm sure he has—'

'That will do, Cee.' James broke in now, and it was obvious he was angry. 'If Morgan is prepared to overlook these allegations, so should you.' He glanced apologetically at Fliss. 'I'm sure you know Bland better than any of us,' he declared firmly. 'And if I were in Morgan's shoes I'd be grateful that you'd found someone like him to turn to. You could have got involved with some scoundrel who would have taken advantage of the situation, believe you me.'

Morgan's lips thinned then, but he didn't argue with his

father, even though Fliss suspected he had more in common
with his mother than James thought. Instead, he let her
excuse herself to make some fresh coffee, and by the time
she returned they had started discussing what he intended
to do now.

Which was how he came to leave when they did, Fliss
remembered broodingly. She wondered if he'd been planning it all along. Well, ever since he'd discovered there
was no challenge in baiting her, she appended tersely. And
asking them to give him a lift back to London had seemed
the most sensible thing to do.

Whether the Rikers had driven him all the way to
Craythorpe she had no way of knowing. Which brought her
back to the problem of how he was now. She had hoped
he might keep in touch, if only to reassure his parents. But,
as Morgan had his own agenda, she couldn't be sure what
he'd told them after they'd left the cottage.

Flicking a hand across the spotless surface of the counter,
Fliss went into the living room now and glanced at the
clock. It was nearly half-past eight, and she had to be at
school for a quarter to nine. She ought to be getting ready
instead of wasting time.

The phone rang as she was starting up the stairs, and,
half believing she had summoned an answer to her problems, she picked up the receiver. 'Yes?' she said, despite
her eagerness having grown a little cautious during the past
week because of the calls she'd been receiving from cranks
and other newspapers who wanted her story. But it was
only Graham on the other end of the line.

'Fliss?' he said, as if there was any doubt of her identity.
'I hoped I'd catch you before you left.' He paused. 'I'm
just returning your call. Can we talk?'

Fliss sighed. 'Well, I'm alone, if that's what you mean,'
she declared, half impatiently. She'd been trying to speak
to Graham all week. But every time she'd rung he was
either out or Mrs Arnold had answered for him, and, as

Fliss had been warned not to tell the housekeeper anything, she'd had to hang up.

'Oh, good.'

Graham sounded pleased, but Fliss was too strung up to share his relief. 'I have to leave in five minutes,' she said, reminding him that she had a job to do, too. 'Why didn't you ring me back last night?'

'I just didn't have the time,' he answered swiftly, but Fliss couldn't help wondering how true that was. He'd had plenty of time to see her in the days before Morgan's return. But, suddenly, he was loaded down with work. 'Was it urgent?'

Fliss took a steadying breath. Urgent enough, she thought painfully, remembering how tearful she'd been the previous evening with the knowledge of another weekend just two days away. She'd wanted to talk to Graham; she'd wanted to feel that he cared about her. But, most of all, she'd wanted to reassure herself that what had happened between her and Morgan had meant nothing to her either.

'I was lonely,' she said now, using James's words, and wishing that that was all that was wrong with her. 'I can't stand not seeing you. Couldn't you pick me up after school? We could drive to Purley reservoir and spend some time alone.'

'Now, Fliss—'

'Now, Fliss—what?' She tried not to sound resentful. 'You know Morgan's not here. I told you last Sunday, when I spoke to you after church. He left with his parents on Saturday afternoon.'

'Well, yes, but—'

'But what? It's not as if I've still got those reporters at the gate. Morgan's gone back to Craythorpe, and I expect they've done the same.' She hesitated. 'I don't think he'll be coming to Whittersley again.'

'You don't?' Although Graham had been dragging his feet before, her words seemed to galvanise his mood. 'Are you saying that he knows about us? That you explained how close we've been? Is he agreeable to you getting a divorce?'

Fliss sighed. 'Well, we didn't get as far as that,' she admitted honestly, wondering if she really knew what Morgan thought about anything. 'But I think he realised that we—that is, that he and I—that our relationship isn't going to work.' Or did he? 'Um, he did sleep in the spare bedroom on Friday night.'

And on Saturday morning…

But she refused to think about that, and, pushing the guilty memories aside, she heard Graham say warmly, 'I never doubted he would.' But she wondered if he meant it; if he hadn't secretly had his doubts. She knew she would in his position, but then, she knew how unreliable she was.

'About this afternoon,' she persisted, glancing at her watch. She really ought to be leaving for work now. But she was sure she'd feel better about everything if she saw him face to face, and there was no earthly reason why they shouldn't meet as friends.

But once again that reluctant note entered Graham's voice, and she knew before he spoke what he was going to say. 'It is a little difficult,' he confessed. 'I've as good as promised Mrs Arnold that I'd take her to Bentbridge to see her sister. You know I'd rather be with you, but—well, is it wise?'

'I don't care if it's wise or not!' exclaimed Fliss half tearfully, aware that her need to see him was self-induced. But she had to get some order back into her life, and that was one thing she could rely on Graham to provide.

'Well…'

He was weakening, and she hurriedly pressed her point. 'Don't I deserve a little of your time?' She glanced at her watch again. She was going to be late. 'Please, Graham. We can't go on like this.'

'Well…' Graham hesitated. 'Perhaps I could meet you,'

he ventured cautiously, and Fliss felt an enormous feeling of relief. 'But I don't think I should pick you up from school in my car. That might cause talk. I think the best thing would be for me to be walking past the gates when you come out. That way, it won't look as if we planned it.'

'Won't it?' Fliss had her doubts, but she didn't have the time to debate it now. 'All right,' she agreed, too relieved that he'd agreed to meet her to say anything to rock the boat. 'I'll be out at a quarter to four. Don't be late.'

'I know what time school gets out,' he declared, half impatiently, and she remembered he was one of the governors, too.

'Okay,' she said. 'I'll look forward to it. But now I've got to go.' She grimaced. 'I'm sure you know what time school starts as well.'

The day dragged. Perhaps it was the fact that she was so eager for it to be over that made the hours go so slowly, and it didn't help when the headmistress called her into her study just after the final bell had gone. Mrs Buxton was inclined to ramble, and Fliss couldn't imagine why she wanted to speak to her anyway. She hoped it wasn't because she'd done something wrong.

'Sit down, Felicity,' her superior directed her pleasantly, clearly unaware that she was eager to leave. But all Fliss could think of was that Graham would be unlikely to wait, and also that he wouldn't be very pleased if she let him down.

Fliss perched on the edge of the chair at the opposite side of the desk, shifting somewhat anxiously as Mrs Buxton took her own seat and shuffled some papers before coming to the point. 'I just thought we should have a little chat, Felicity,' she said pleasantly. 'Not about your work,' she added understandingly. 'We're very happy with that.'

Fliss was grateful for small mercies, but she wished Mrs Buxton would get on. It was after a quarter to four already, and Graham might think he'd missed her when she didn't appear.

'No, it's about your husband coming home,' explained the headmistress, setting her papers aside and putting the cap back on her pen. 'I've sounded out some of the governors and they agree with me: we feel we ought to grant you some—what shall we call it?—compassionate leave?'

Fliss swallowed. 'Com—passionate leave?'

Mrs Buxton nodded. 'I think it's the least we can do in the circumstances,' she declared. 'I was reading about the honorary award the Nyandan government are going to offer him at their millennium celebrations in the newspaper this morning. I'm sure you know the circumstances better than me, but I want you to know that we're all very happy for you.'

'Thank you.'

Fliss hoped she didn't look as blank as she was feeling at that moment. An award, she thought stupidly. What award?

'Anyway,' went on the other woman chummily, 'I know it's going to be very exciting having your husband home again. I realise you must have a hundred things to talk about, but perhaps, after he's had time to settle down again, you might be able to persuade him to come and speak to the school.'

Ah! Fliss was beginning to understand. The governors—not Graham, she was sure, but some of the others—were not just thinking of her. They were hoping that a visit from Morgan might bring some welcome publicity to the school.

'Well—' she began, but Mrs Buxton must have seen the doubt in her face and quickly forestalled her.

'Don't say anything more now,' she said. 'I'm sure you need a little time to think it over. But—quality time is so important. We just want you to enjoy the relief of having him home.'

Quality time!

Fliss knew a hysterical desire to laugh. She wondered what Mrs Buxton would say if she told her they had already had some 'quality time' together, and it had resulted in Morgan walking out of the house.

But all she said was, 'Thank you,' again, before getting gratefully to her feet. With a bit of luck, Graham might not have deserted her, and at least the delay meant the children had all had time to disperse.

'I'll see you tomorrow,' Mrs Buxton promised, and Fliss offered her a polite smile as she started for the door. But, as she went out into the corridor, she reminded herself that she would have to start reading the newspapers again. If Mrs Buxton knew Morgan was going to be offered an honorary award so should she.

The schoolyard was deserted, as she'd expected, with only Mrs Buxton's car still residing in its space beside the wall. She thought at first that there was no sign of Graham either, but then she saw him standing across the road, talking to one of his parishioners.

She crossed the schoolyard briskly, buttoning her jacket as she walked. It was still breezy, but the wind was milder, and she'd worn the jacket deliberately because the rich green fabric flattered her colouring.

Graham saw her at once, and she slowed her pace as he obviously made an effort to excuse himself from his companion. But the woman was tenacious, laying a hand on his arm when he would have turned away. Whatever it was she was saying, she considered it important, and Fliss could only hope it was nothing to do with her.

She started up the High Street, heading towards her cottage which was situated at the end, near the churchyard. Too late, she wondered if it wouldn't have been wiser to walk towards the village stores. That way, Graham would have had longer to extricate himself from the woman's chatter.

But in the event it wasn't necessary. She had only cov-

ered a few yards when she heard Graham's laboured
breathing behind her. He was panting quite badly as he
came abreast of her, and she promised herself to speak to
Mrs Arnold about all those stodgy meals.

'I thought you must be avoiding me,' he said, when he'd
got his breath back, and Fliss couldn't help but be irritated
by his words.

'As if,' she said shortly. 'Mrs Buxton wanted to speak
to me. She'd apparently spoken to some of the governors
about giving me some compassionate leave.'

'Oh, yes.'

Graham nodded, and Fliss gasped, 'You mean you
knew?'

'Well, it was mooted at Tuesday's governors' meeting,'
he agreed. 'I could hardly object without drawing attention
to myself.'

'And that would never do,' said Fliss bitterly, and then
wished she hadn't when he gave her a wounded look. 'Oh,
I'm sorry, but all this talk about Morgan coming home is
getting to me. I can hardly tell everyone that he's been and
gone.'

'No.' But Graham looked happier now. 'Well, you can
always say he's staying with his parents for the time being.
They'll understand. Anyone with any imagination at all will
know it can't be easy. As you say, we've known one another longer than you'd known him.'

'Yes.' But Fliss wasn't so sanguine about the situation.
She couldn't help remembering that Morgan had made no
promises when he left. Until he'd found a job and a home,
she didn't think she'd rest easy. She bit her lip. 'Did you
know the Nyandan government want to give him an
award?'

'A millennium medal!' said Graham disparagingly. His
lips drew in again. 'Yes, I did see something about it in
the press.' He shook his head. 'It always amuses me how

these people love to glorify their achievements. I mean, this President Mdola was just a rebel a few months ago.'

Fliss hesitated. 'I—don't think Morgan has tried to glorify himself,' she ventured reluctantly. She might have no respect for him herself, but she couldn't let Graham run him down. 'He—well, I know he prefers not to talk about it. Getting him to say anything about his experiences is like pulling teeth.'

Graham sniffed. 'Well, if you say so. But I wasn't actually criticising your husband, you know. It's this man, Mdola, I was referring to. Despite what anyone says, he's just another little dictator who's puffed up with his own success.'

Fliss blew out a breath. 'He is organising democratic elections,' she pointed out equably.

'Democratic elections!' Graham was sceptical. 'And how far will this new-found democracy go?'

'As far as it takes,' remarked a sardonic voice behind them, and Fliss uttered a gasp and swung round to find Morgan blocking the path.

CHAPTER TEN

SHE didn't know who was the more shocked, herself or Graham. Her husband was the last person either of them had expected to see. But she supposed she should have been warned that she hadn't seen the back of him. No matter how he'd treated her, he simply wasn't the kind of man to give her up without a fight. Even if he didn't want her himself, she speculated. There was far too much fun to be had in making her eat her words.

He looked a lot different from the last time she'd seen him. His hair was slowly growing back, and the silvery fairness that was evident was a complete contrast to his dark skin. He'd shaved off his beard, and his dark suit and long black overcoat looked far more expensive than the rough trousers and sweater the air force had provided. He looked—good, she admitted, though that adjective was barely adequate. Damn him, he looked very attractive, and far too disturbing to her peace of mind.

'You must be Graham Bland,' Morgan was saying now, turning to the other man and holding out his hand. 'The *Reverend* Graham Bland; isn't that what you told me, Fliss?' he added, as Graham responded. The two men shook hands. 'I want to thank you for looking after my wife while I've been away.'

Fliss wanted to die, and she thought Graham probably had similar feelings, but so long as Morgan was being polite there was little he could do. 'I—it was my pleasure,' he muttered, and Morgan's lips tightened.

'I'll bet,' he said, in a dangerously bland tone. 'Were you coming to the cottage?'

'No.' Graham was very definite about that and Fliss won-

dered if he realised how flustered he looked. She'd always
thought his dog collar suited his rather heavy features, but
now it seemed too tight for comfort and his face was quite
red. 'I—no,' he said again. 'Fliss was just coming out of
school as I was passing. I'm on my way to the vicarage.
My housekeeper is expecting me for tea.'

'Oh, that's a shame.' They had reached the cottage gate
now and Fliss reached clumsily for the latch. 'I was looking
forward to hearing more of your views about the situation
in Nyanda,' Morgan continued pleasantly. 'It's interesting
to know how people like yourself think.'

'It is?'

Graham's voice was a little hoarse now, and Fliss had to
stifle the urge to scream. Couldn't he see that Morgan was
only baiting him? she wondered irritably. Pushing open the
gate, she left them to it and started up the path.

'Cheerio, Fliss.'

Graham's farewell drifted after her, and she turned to lift
her hand in a reluctant wave. She almost lost her courage
when she discovered that Morgan was right behind her, but
she refused to let him see how spooked she was.

She could imagine how Graham was feeling as he left
them. Heavens, it was only that morning that she'd been
telling him she didn't think she'd see Morgan again. Well,
not in Whittersley, she amended, speculating that she would
have had to see him again if she wanted a divorce. But
even that seemed remote in the present situation.

Deciding there was no point in attempting to talk to
Morgan outside, she unlocked the door and led the way
into the cottage. She got a not altogether pleasant sense of
déjà vu as he closed the door behind him, but she determined to be positive this time and not let him get under
her skin.

'I guess you weren't best pleased to see me,' he remarked as she bustled about, taking off her jacket and setting a tumbled cushion to rights. 'I suppose, in your opin-

ion, I couldn't have appeared at a more inconvenient moment. I must say, you two haven't wasted any time before resuming your affair.'

Fliss, who had been examining her reflection in the mirror that hung over the corner bookcase, now turned with an angry splash of colour in her cheeks. But then, remembering the promise she'd made to herself, she schooled her features. 'We were never having an affair,' she replied coolly, 'so there wasn't one to resume.'

'So you say.'

'So I know,' she retorted, stung by his scepticism. She took a deep breath. 'Is that why you came back? To try and catch us out?'

'No.' Morgan had the grace to look a little discomfited. But his eyes darkened. 'It's not my fault if you can't control yourselves.' He paused. 'As a matter of fact, I came to tell you I'll be starting work as soon as the medic thinks I'm fit.'

'Starting work?' Fliss stared at him. 'D'you mean they've offered you a job at the base?'

'I didn't go back to Craythorpe,' replied Morgan, lifting his shoulders carelessly. 'I've been staying with a friend since I left here.'

'A friend?' Fliss felt her stomach hollow. 'What friend?' There were a number of female acquaintances that instantly came to mind as well as the more likely male ones. Not least, Cheryl Lewis, who, even before her divorce from Doug, had made no secret of her attraction to Fliss's husband.

'Does it matter?' Morgan asked now, and she guessed he was enjoying her curiosity. 'The point of this story is that I've been staying in London. There was no sense in going back to Craythorpe when there was nothing more they could do.'

'Is that your decision or theirs?' Fliss could hear the tartness of her tone and resented his ability to make her sound like a shrew. 'Anyway—' she took another steadying breath '—I'm pleased for you. Um—you didn't tell me what you were going to do.'

'No. So I didn't.' For a moment, she thought he was going to leave her in the dark. He hesitated. 'You remember I told you I'd kept a journal while I was in captivity? Well, Gerry Grant is interested. He thinks he'll be able to sell it if I can turn it into a book.'

'Gerry Grant!' Fliss was impressed. At the time Morgan was trying to sell his first book, the literary agent who represented a string of successful writers had turned him down.

'Yeah. I was surprised, too,' Morgan added, 'but you'd be surprised what a little publicity will do. He contacted me after reading about my experiences in the press. When he heard I'd been keeping a journal, he seemed quite keen to offer me a deal.'

Fliss swallowed. 'That's great.'

'You don't sound as if it is.'

'Oh, I do.' Fliss didn't want him to think she was bitter, or jealous of his success. But she wondered what he'd say if she told him that she'd had to return the advance on his first book to Marius Blake when its publication had fallen through. That was one of the reasons why she'd found it easier to move out of London. Her experiences with publishers had left her wary, to say the least. 'How—how did he know where you were?'

'I believe he rang Craythorpe and someone there gave him my number,' replied Morgan. 'I had to keep the doctor informed of my whereabouts. That was one of the conditions of letting me leave the base.'

Fliss frowned. 'What were the others?'

'Nothing important.' Morgan shrugged his shoulders. 'I'm supposed to eat lots of wholesome food, get to bed early, and avoid alcohol. Apart from an occasional lapse…' his lips twisted, and she wondered what particular lapse he was thinking about '…I've tried to do as I was told.'

'I'm sure.' Once again, Fliss could hear the asperity in her voice, and she struggled to find something positive to say. 'It sounds as if you've been busy.' She linked her fingers together. 'Um—have you found somewhere to live, too?'

'Other than where I've been living, you mean?' Morgan seemed amused at her enquiry. She guessed he'd sensed that she was really curious, and she knew a sudden urge to wipe that smug expression off his face. 'Well, yes. I've managed to find myself a small apartment. It's not as comfortable as a house, of course, but it will do for the time being.'

'Is it in central London?'

Fliss knew how expensive renting in central London could be, but it wasn't until she'd voiced the question that she realised how nosy it was. But, dammit, she had a right to know where he was living, even if the wry acknowledgement in his eyes caused her conscience some confusion.

'It's not in London at all,' he responded at last, evidently prepared to humour her. 'I find I don't like the place as much as I did. Perhaps I've got used to somewhere quieter. I've decided I need somewhere less hectic to work.'

'I see.'

Fliss didn't know if he was being deliberately evasive, but once again he'd avoided a direct answer. When she came to think of it, he'd replied to few of her questions directly, and, while he might argue that it was none of her business, she was tempted to ask him why, in that case, he'd bothered to come.

On top of which, he'd spoiled one of the few occasions she'd had to talk to Graham privately, although, if she was honest, she would admit she hadn't thought of it at the time. She'd been too afraid of what Morgan might do to the other man, but it seemed she'd been overreacting there, too.

So what did Morgan want?

After the way he'd treated Graham, she didn't flatter herself that he'd had second thoughts about what had happened the morning before he left. Not that she wanted him to, she berated herself, despite the latent awareness he aroused in her. The way she'd reacted that morning was a source of much embarrassment to her, and, however often she tried to tell herself that it had just been a mindless urge to mate with a virile male, she was not convinced.

Her breath caught. But she had to convince herself, she thought fiercely, heading into the kitchen to avoid further grief. She'd betrayed her conscience and she'd betrayed Graham. Admitting, even if it was only to herself, that Morgan still disturbed her sexually was only playing into his hands.

She had put the kettle on to boil and was staring out at the daffodils again when Morgan came to the door of the kitchen. She was just thinking how tight-lipped she looked, reflected in the window, and she decided she resented his assumption that he could come here when he liked.

'What are you doing?'

Morgan propped his shoulder against the door frame and stood regarding her consideringly, and she wondered what his answer would be if she said 'Avoiding you!' But, despite her indignation, she found she couldn't say something like that. The trouble was, every time she looked at him she kept seeing him as he'd been that morning before he'd humiliated her. And, no matter how she tried to banish the image, it just wouldn't go away.

Consequently, her voice was a little husky when she said, 'What does it look like I'm doing?' She cleared her throat. 'I'm making tea.' She glanced over her shoulder. 'Do you want some?'

'Aren't you going to ask me where I'm going to live?' he asked irritatingly, and she boosted her anger at him by observing that, once again, he'd avoided answering her.

'No,' she said now, deciding she wouldn't demean herself by playing his games. 'Do you want tea or not?'

Morgan took a resigned breath. 'Why do I get the feeling that you're angry with me?' he asked mildly. 'I thought you'd be pleased to hear that I'm getting on with my life.'

If only...

Fliss's hands were balled into fists as she turned to face him. 'Why should you imagine I'd be interested in anything you plan to do?' she demanded, hiding her hands behind her back, and he choked back a laugh.

'Maybe because of all the questions you've been asking since I got here?' he suggested, when he'd recovered his composure. 'Come on, Fliss. You're just annoyed because I haven't come crawling back here with my tail between my legs.'

'That's not true.'

'Isn't it?'

'No.' She heard the kettle boiling behind her and swung round impatiently to turn it off. 'I just don't know why you have come back. After the way you—you behaved before you left, I'd have thought I was the last person you'd want to see again.'

'Would you?' Morgan regarded her between narrowed lids, and in spite of all her efforts her pulse quickened at that sensual appraisal. 'Well, you could be right about that.'

'Then—'

'I had something to give you,' he declared abruptly, as if he, too, was not appreciating the sudden intimacy that had developed between them. He put his hand into his inside pocket and pulled out an envelope. 'This is yours, I believe.'

Fliss took the envelope reluctantly, making sure she avoided touching his fingers in the process. It wasn't difficult. It was a business-size envelope and he handed it to her without ceremony. With a fleeting glance at him, she slipped her finger under the flap and slit it across.

She didn't know what she expected. Some kind of official communication, she supposed. Maybe the notification he'd received about being given an award, although she couldn't see how that might belong to her. Maybe he'd been to see a solicitor, and this was a petition for divorce, she speculated with an aching throat, but she didn't think even he could be that cruel.

It was a cheque.

For a moment, Fliss thought there'd been some mistake; that he'd given her an envelope intended for someone else. Even so, she was astounded that he had so much money to give away. And then she saw her name as the payee, and her mouth went unpleasantly dry.

'What is this?'

'To use your own words: what does it look like?' he countered. 'It's a cheque. You deposit it in the bank.'

'I can see it's a cheque.' Fliss stared at him with wary eyes. 'What I meant was, what's it for?'

'It's for you,' said Morgan flatly, and this time there was no equivocation in his words. 'Don't you think it's adequate? I thought it was quite generous myself.'

'You bastard!'

Pain, hot and heavy, flooded through her. She'd thought he couldn't do anything else to humiliate her. But she was wrong. He wasn't finished with her yet.

She flung the cheque towards him, but it was too light to reach its target and merely fluttered, aimlessly, to the floor. When he bent to pick it up, she was tempted to bring one of her fists down on his head. But, in spite of everything, she couldn't bring herself to inflict the pain.

'Fliss—'

His exasperated use of her name was the last straw, however. 'Get out of here,' she said. 'Just take your filthy money and go.'

'For God's sake, Fliss—' He was less tolerant now.

'Have you taken leave of your senses? What the hell are you so riled up about? What am I supposed to have done?'

'You don't know?' Her lips curled. 'My God, I knew you'd changed, Morgan, but I didn't realise how much. I was prepared to accept that your experiences must have had some effect on you, but don't think you can practise the law of the jungle around here!'

'The law of the jungle!' Although there was incredulity in his voice, he was beginning to sound annoyed now, and she felt a certain amount of satisfaction for knowing the tables had been turned. 'You don't know anything about the jungle,' he added harshly. 'But if you're trying to provoke me, carry on.'

Fliss shook her head. 'I've said all I want to say,' she declared stiffly, but when he continued to stare at her she lost her nerve. 'Just go,' she said, brushing past him into the living room. The kitchen was too small, she thought. There was nowhere to run.

He let her go, but he came after her, blocking any chance she might have had to open the outer door. Despite the fact that he was leaner than he used to be, he moved with an agile athleticism, creating an immovable obstacle in her path.

She wasn't afraid, Fliss told herself. Though the memory of what had happened the last time they had had a confrontation was rather obviously at the front of her mind. She couldn't forget that she had been as much to blame for his loss of control as he had. It was an unacceptable admission, but it was true.

'Are you going?' she demanded, taking refuge in anger.

'Not yet,' he responded civilly, but there was a dangerous light sparkling in his eyes. 'I'm still waiting for you to explain what the hell you're talking about. You can't accuse me of having some ulterior motive for giving you money and then not tell me what it is I'm supposed to have done.'

'Well, I'm going to have a bath,' she said, refusing to

answer him. She decided she'd feel safer behind a locked door. 'I shall expect you to be gone when I come down.'

Morgan shrugged as she went somewhat defiantly towards the stairs, but he made no move to leave. He just stood there, watching her, his coat pushed aside and his hands shoved carelessly into his jacket pockets. If she didn't know better, she'd have said he was completely indifferent to what she did, and she resented feeling an interloper in her own home.

Determined not to let him upset her, she went firmly up the stairs, balancing her feet on every tread. She wouldn't admit to going slower than she usually did, but she knew she was, entering her bedroom with an undeniable sense of unease. Dammit, had he only come here to insult her? What else could he possibly want?

The answer was obvious, she thought bitterly. He'd come back to finish what he'd started last weekend, but she'd disconcerted him by her reaction to his—*generosity*. How could he? she wondered, with a shiver. Did he think she was so short of funds she'd do anything for money?

She swallowed painfully, staring without satisfaction at her reflection in the dressing table mirror. Had she changed so much that he thought he had only to wave a cheque beneath her nose to get her to jump into bed with him? Was she so desperate for attention that she'd conveyed that impression to him?

Surely not.

She blew out a tremulous breath. Well, whatever he thought, it wasn't true, she told herself. She had Graham. She loved Graham and he loved her. He'd never have treated her the way Morgan had treated her—

Her thoughts were abruptly curtailed by the realisation that her husband's image had joined hers in the mirror. While she had been assuring herself of Graham's worthiness, Morgan had come silently up the stairs and was now standing in the bedroom doorway. He was still wearing his overcoat, she noticed, but his hands weren't in his pockets now. They were supporting his weight at either side of the open doorway as he stood regarding her with enquiring eyes.

'I thought you were going to take a bath.'

Fliss sucked in a breath. So that was it. He'd assumed she'd be in the bathroom by now, and he'd decided to come and take a look. What had he intended to do? she wondered. Hadn't she made her position clear enough before?

'I am going to take a bath,' she said now, coldly. 'What do you want to do?' Her lips curled. 'Join me?'

'It's a thought,' he replied quietly, his eyes drifting appraisingly over her unyielding figure. 'But, actually, I wanted to explain that cheque to you. I find I can't walk out of here until I do.'

Fliss stiffened. 'I don't think any explanation is necessary.'

'Well, I do.' He pushed himself away from the door, his hands falling loosely to his sides. 'I finally worked out what you must have thought it was and I wanted to assure you that, however sexually deprived I might feel, I haven't yet succumbed to the need to pay for my pleasures.'

Fliss's expression didn't change. 'It didn't take you long to come up with an excuse, then,' she said scornfully. 'You'll be telling me next that you regret making a fool of me last weekend.'

Morgan shrugged. 'Perhaps I do.'

'Oh, come on...' She swung round abruptly, unable to go on talking to a reflection when the man himself was right behind her. 'You enjoyed humiliating me. Admit it. You just wanted to prove that you still had some—some power over me.'

'That's not true.' His response was automatic, but his mouth had tightened again and she thought she was closer to the truth than he cared to admit. Then he sighed. 'Well, all right. Maybe there was an element of power in it, but it wasn't just you who was humiliated. It was me, too.'

'You!' Patently, she didn't believe him.

'Yes, me.' He approached the bed. 'May I?' He indicated the fact that he'd like to sit down, and because he looked a little pale suddenly she nodded. He sank down onto the mattress. 'I guess I'm not the stud I thought I was.'

Fliss caught her breath. 'You're not serious.'

'Why not?' He rested back on his hands and looked up at her. 'I hesitate to mention it again, but Jamara wasn't a holiday camp, you know.'

'Even so...'

'Even so, what?' He gave a wry grimace. 'I haven't slept with a woman for over four years. Don't you think that's quite daunting? Perhaps I've lost the knack.'

Fliss hadn't known whether to believe him or not, but now his deliberate attempt to trivialise the situation persuaded her that this was just another attempt on his part to gain her sympathy. 'Why don't you just give me the reason you've cooked up for handing me that cheque and we'll call it a day?' she asked tersely. 'I'm not angry any longer, I'm just tired. I want you to go.'

Morgan lowered himself back against the coverlet and withdrew the cheque from his pocket once again. 'Look at it,' he said, handing it to her. 'Look at the amount. Isn't it at all familiar to you?'

Fliss took the cheque reluctantly, but she didn't have to look at it again to know how much it was for. It was engraved on her mind. 'No,' she said crisply. 'It means nothing to me.'

'Then it should,' he retorted impatiently. 'It's the advance—plus interest—that Marius Blake paid for *Nightshift*.'

Fliss's jaw dropped. 'I don't believe it—' she was beginning, when her eyes dropped to the signature on the cheque. It meant nothing, but below it was printed the publisher's name in small black letters. 'Oh, God!'

CHAPTER ELEVEN

MORGAN'S lean features looked a little less drawn. 'Is that an apology?'

Fliss shook her head. She couldn't speak at first, but when she found her voice she said helplessly, 'Why didn't you tell me?'

'I tried to,' he reminded her drily, and she expelled a guilty sigh.

'Oh, God,' she said again. 'I'm sorry.' And then, seating herself beside him on the bed, she added, 'But I don't want this. It—it's yours.'

'No, it's yours,' he contradicted her softly. 'I went to see Marius yesterday morning and he had to confess that he'd made you repay the advance.' He closed his eyes for a moment against the anguish he was feeling. 'That was why you had to get rid of the car, wasn't it? And the house; although I'd like to think that was more because you felt some reluctance to go on living in the home we'd shared.' He opened his eyes again. 'Why the hell didn't you tell me?'

'How could I?' Fliss was rueful now. 'I didn't know he was going to develop a conscience and refund the money, did I?'

'And he hasn't,' said Morgan wryly, unfastening the top two buttons of his shirt and pulling his tie away from his collar. 'That's better,' he added. Then he said, 'Marius is no bleeding heart, Fliss. He's a businessman, first and foremost, but even he can see the potential for publishing a book of mine now. It may not have a great deal of relevance to what happened to me in Nyanda, but it does have the advantage of beating that book onto the shelves.'

Fliss stared at him. 'The rat!'

Morgan grinned. 'Well, at least he's paid rather handsomely for the privilege. Together with the advance Gerry's negotiating for the new book, I should be fairly well off.'

Fliss pressed her lips together. 'I'm pleased for you.'

'You sound as if you mean it now.'

'I meant it before.'

'Did you?' He shrugged, but she sensed he was keeping his scepticism to himself. 'Well, at least you know I wasn't trying to insult you.'

'Hmm.' Fliss nodded. Then, because she couldn't deny that she was still concerned about him, she added, 'So how are you? Really, I mean.'

'Do you care?'

'Yes, I do care.' Fliss sighed. 'What did you eventually tell your parents? I haven't heard from them either since you left.'

Morgan frowned. 'Well, they were concerned,' he conceded. 'And I guess my leaving when they did persuaded them that things were not the same between us.'

Fliss felt terrible. 'What must they think of me?'

'Does it matter?' Morgan was rather cynical. 'If we're not going to stay together, they have to know.'

Fliss supposed he was right, but there was something so final about his logic. Was that how he felt, too? Did he have no misgivings? Or was his determination to get on with his life an indication that he had no regrets?

'Anyway, they dropped me off in London,' Morgan was continuing now. 'Paul—Paul Giles, that is—had contacted me while I was at Craythorpe, and he'd offered me a bed for a few nights if I needed a base. He knew you were living in Whittersley, and he guessed I'd want to renew my contacts in town.'

'I see.'

Fliss was relieved. At least she knew where he'd been staying now. She might not like his former boss and his wife, but that wasn't important. It was good to know there wasn't another woman in his life.

Why?

But that particular yawning chasm was not one she cared to explore right now, and, to distract herself, she returned to what she'd said before. 'I've been worried about you,' she admitted. 'I didn't know where you were or what you were doing. And there was no one I could get in touch with to find out.'

'You could have rung Mum and Dad.'

'I could.'

But Fliss didn't look convinced, and he pulled a face. 'You could have,' he insisted. 'They would have probably been sympathetic. Particularly if you'd told them I was impotent, as well.'

Fliss caught her breath. 'You're not impotent!'

Morgan regarded her through narrowed lids. 'Would it bother you if I was?'

Fliss stared at him. 'Don't be silly,' she said. And then, as a trace of anguish crossed his face, she added, 'Of course it would.'

'Why?'

'Why?' Fliss's throat was suddenly dry. 'What kind of a question is that?'

'A fairly straightforward one, I'd have said,' he responded flatly, sitting up again. 'Don't you like plain speaking?'

'That's not plain speaking,' protested Fliss uneasily. 'I—you—whatever gave you that idea anyway?'

'You did,' said Morgan, raking a hand over his scalp. His hair was more than just stubble now, and she realised that in no time it would be as thick as it had ever been. 'Why'd you think I didn't—?'

He broke off, but she knew exactly what he meant, and she stared at him disbelievingly. 'You said—you said you didn't want to sleep with—'

'I know what I said,' he interrupted her harshly. 'But the truth is, I was afraid I couldn't do it, so I blamed you.'

Fliss couldn't believe it. 'That can't be true,' she said unsteadily, and Morgan gave her a twisted smile.

'Well, we'll never know, will we?' he remarked, running his palms over the edge of the mattress. 'I guess this is where I came in.'

'No, it's not.' When he would have pushed himself to his feet, Fliss gripped his arm. 'Morgan, you can't just walk out of here after saying something like that. For pity's sake, what happened to you?'

Morgan bent his head. 'Nothing happened to me.'

'But it must have done. Unless...' She caught her lower lip between her teeth. 'Unless it's a psychological thing.'

'Yeah. That's probably what it is,' he said, blowing out a breath. 'Anyway, it's my problem, not yours.'

Fliss wished that were true, but the fact was, she still felt a certain amount of responsibility for the way Morgan was feeling now. He was her husband, she thought unsteadily, and it wasn't his fault that he'd been reported dead and she'd found someone else.

For a fleeting moment the thought of Graham brought a measure of sanity. What would he have her do in these circumstances? Certainly not what she was thinking of doing, she thought ruefully, but although she knew she owed her allegiance to him she still cared about Morgan. She couldn't ignore his pain any more than she could ignore her own.

'You're not impotent,' she told him carefully, taking one of his hands between both of hers. She expelled a breath. 'I know it.'

'How do you know it?'

Morgan was looking disbelievingly at her now, and although she suspected she wasn't equipped to handle a situation like this she forced herself to go on. 'Because you're not,' she assured him, conscious of the cool strength of the fingers between her palms. 'You forget: I've had first-hand experience.'

'Big deal!' Morgan was sardonic. 'Fliss, it's been a long time since you and I—well, you know what I mean.' He put her hands aside and got to his feet. 'Anyway, thanks for the endorsement. It's good to know that one of us has some faith in me.'

Fliss looked helplessly up at him. 'This isn't helping, you know,' she said. 'Can't we at least talk about this? Can't you stay?'

Morgan sighed. 'A few minutes ago, you wanted to get rid of me,' he reminded her.

'I know that.' Fliss hesitated. 'I didn't mean it.' She tugged his sleeve. 'I'd really like us to talk.'

Morgan tipped his head back on his shoulders. 'What about?'

'I don't know.' She was troubled. 'I guess we need to talk about us.'

'Us?' He came down on the bed again rather heavily. 'Fliss, there is no us. You know that as well as me.'

Fliss took a deep breath. 'We can still be friends, can't we?'

'Friends?' She was devastated by the depth of raw emotion in his gaze. 'Fliss, you and I can never be friends, and you know it. Now, cut this out, and let me get out of here.'

She knew he was right. She knew that her amateur attempt at counselling was in danger of backfiring on her, but she couldn't let him go. When he'd sat down again, he'd left barely an inch of space between them, and she was experiencing the craziest urge to lean against his arm.

'Fliss.'

He said her name half defeatedly, but the husky timbre of his voice reverberated down to her toes. It couldn't help but remind her of all the other times he'd made love to her, and although she was sure she was going to regret it later she lifted her hand and turned his face towards her.

'Morgan...'

'No.' His voice was harsh. 'No, don't say anything, Fliss, it's over. You can tell Bland I said that he's a lucky man.'

If anything had been able to deter her, it should have been that. She was fairly sure he had used Graham's name deliberately in a vain attempt to prevent her from doing something rash. But the anguish in his eyes was causing a sympathetic quickening of her heartbeat, and she was fascinated by the sensual beauty of his mouth.

'Morgan,' she said again, her fingertips invading the soft growth of ash-blond hair behind his ears. She found she was actually revelling in the power she sensed she had over him, and she moistened her lips, which were soft and parted. 'Can I kiss you?' And when he didn't move away she said, 'I'll take that as a yes.'

His mouth was hard but it yielded beneath the urgent pressure of hers and it took little effort to propel him back onto the satin coverlet. For the first time in her life, she felt as if she was in charge of their lovemaking, and there was a heady delight in initiating what came next. Her tongue slipped easily between his teeth, sliding along the length of his in sensuous invitation. If he had had any doubts about her commitment to what she was doing, then surely they must have been dissipated, she thought breathlessly. If she had her way, he'd soon be as eager to participate as she was herself.

She knew he was holding himself in check at the moment, but whether that was because he was prepared to let her make all the running, or because he was still reluctant to test his powers, she couldn't be sure. The only thing she was sure of was that as she continued to cover his face with feather-light kisses his responses began to change.

To begin with, his hand came up, almost of its own volition, to cup the back of her head, securing her mouth to his. His long fingers moved impatiently among the loops of her braid and she wasn't really surprised when her hair tumbled untidily about her shoulders a few moments later. His hand slid into the silky coils then, and she thought she heard him give a muffled groan as she moved against him.

'You're overdressed,' he muttered, the words practically torn from him, and Fliss knew an overwhelming feeling of satisfaction.

'So are you,' she breathed, trying to push his coat and his suit jacket off his shoulders, and was pleasantly surprised when he let her help him ease them off. 'That's much better,' she murmured, pulling his tie free and loosening the other buttons on his shirt. She took an unsteady breath at the sight of his brown torso. 'Much better.'

She dipped her head to his chest, nibbling at his taut nipples in much the same way as he used to nibble at hers. He was amazingly sensitive to the caressing brush of her tongue, and his breathing quickened in protest when her fingers moved to his belt.

'Wait!'

'Why?' Her eyes felt heavy with emotion. 'Don't you like what I'm doing?'

'Stop it,' he said, almost harshly. 'You know what I'm talking about.'

'Oh…' She pretended to misunderstand him. 'You're objecting because I'm still fully dressed, is that it?' She didn't wait for his denial, but hurried on, 'Well, that's easily remedied.' She hooked her hands beneath the hem of her sweater and pulled it over her head, exposing her lacy bra. 'That's better, isn't it?'

'No—'

'Of course it is.' She hesitated only a moment before releasing the catch on her bra and pulling it forward over her arms. 'That's much better.'

Morgan closed his eyes against the sensual appeal of her breasts. Full and rounded, the nipples dark and swollen, they were an irresistible temptation to any man, and despite his protests she was reassured when he looped one hand at the back of her neck and pulled her down to him. His mouth was hot against her skin, and a ripple of pure delight ran through her when he brought one of her breasts to his mouth. He suckled hungrily, his tongue inciting every nerve and sinew, and her head fell back in helpless wonder at the ability he had to pleasure her. She could feel the heat of his mouth spreading its message down into her thighs, and between her legs a pulse was beating.

Her hands sought his belt again, and although she sensed that he was still reluctant to let her undress him fully he didn't stop her this time. And why should he? she wondered tremulously, feeling the swollen pressure of his erection straining his zip. She couldn't wait to take him into her hands, and her fingers fumbled with the button at the waistband of his trousers before she succeeded in dragging the zip down. Silk boxers were no barrier to her seeking hands, and her fingers slipped eagerly under the waistband and pushed them down his legs.

He was so hot; that was her first thought. Hot, and smooth, and silky, and pulsing heavily beneath her hand. Her fingers deliberately slid along his length and Morgan groaned in protest. 'Fliss,' he muttered, his breathing laboured, but she wasn't about to give up now.

'Let me,' she said, quickly disposing of her skirt and tights before she had second thoughts. 'There; isn't that nice?' she asked, straddling him possessively. She was on a high that was only rocked a little when Morgan's hands came to caress her bare behind.

She bucked a little nervously when his fingers found the sensitive cleft between her buttocks. She was aware that he thought she was an experienced woman, but the truth was she hadn't been with any other man but him. She might have wished Graham were more forthcoming in that direction, but she was grateful now that he hadn't let her break her vows.

'Fliss...'

Morgan had his eyes closed now, and she could see the film of perspiration on his brow. She guessed he was probably as nervous as she was, though why he should be in the present circumstances she couldn't imagine.

'Ah, Fliss…' His thumbs found the moist curls between her legs, and parted the soft folds to find the swollen nub she couldn't hide. Just the brush of his fingers and she was lost to all reason, her thighs quivering uncontrollably as she jerked against his hand.

She was ashamed then of how swiftly she had climaxed. What kind of a woman would he think she was to have so little control over her needs? She was doing this for him, not to give herself a thrill, she chided. But the ripples of feeling just went on and on.

'Good?' he asked, opening his eyes, and for the first time she was self-conscious about her nudity.

'Good,' she nodded hastily, looking down at his body to avoid his eyes. But when she would have guided him into her moist sheath he held her back.

'It's not going to work,' he said hoarsely, his hand gripping her wrist. 'Fliss, I'm happy for you, really I am, but that's as far as it goes.'

'No—'

She bent over him then, offering her breasts to his protesting mouth. He might have wanted to refuse, but he couldn't resist their bounty, and as he took one dark-circled nipple into his mouth she moved onto him.

His rejection was instantaneous, but it was too late then. His length was encased in a honeycomb of muscle that contracted around him when he would have pulled away.

'God, Fliss—'

His eyes were wide now, wide and oddly vulnerable. If she hadn't known better, she'd have thought this was all new to him, and when the satisfying thickness of his erection started to fade she realised what she had to do. She had to prove to him that he was still the man he had always been, and to do that she had to make love to him.

He moaned when she let him slip out of her, and his anguish was evident when she bent her head to his thighs. For some reason, best known to himself, he had lost his faith in his own masculinity. He hadn't been lying to her. He really was afraid he couldn't satisfy her or himself.

And then she saw it.

She hadn't noticed it before, but that was hardly surprising. She'd been too intent on proving she could take control of their lovemaking to pay too much attention to his limbs. It was another scar, she saw. Not like the other one that formed a jagged line across his abdomen. This scar was small and round and ugly. A savage blemish on the skin of his inner thigh.

It looked like—and probably was—a bullet hole, she decided, and her lips parted in disbelief. An inch, that was all; another inch, and it would have castrated him. Dear God, was that why he was so afraid of sex?

But she couldn't let him know what she was thinking, she realised. Even though she deliberately put her lips to his scorched flesh. Despite his efforts to deter her, she had to go through with this. She *wanted* to go through with it. She wanted to prove to him, once and for all, that he had nothing to fear.

'Fliss!'

He tried to stop her when she started to arouse him, when she used her lips and tongue to excite him, but there was nothing he could do about it. The fact that his ankles were confined by his trousers restricted his opposition, and his hands groped for handfuls of her hair without success.

'For God's sake,' he muttered, but she wasn't listening to him. Under her tender ministrations, he was fast approaching his own climax and she was delighted. But before that happened she straddled him again.

She rode him eagerly, memories of other occasions when

she had done this returning to give her confidence that she'd succeed. And she knew she'd achieved her objective when his hands clutched her to him, and he rolled over to imprison her beneath him as she climaxed again.

Morgan followed her. She felt the flooding warmth of his ejaculation only seconds after her own release, and his shuddering body collapsed in her arms. Even then, little contractions of her muscles continued to tighten around him, and he jerked several more times before he was still.

When he finally drew away, it was she who protested, but he swung his legs over the side of the bed and sat up. 'Thanks,' he said, with a brief glance over his shoulder. Then he got up and pulled up his shorts and trousers before fastening his zip.

'Hey...' She was a little unnerved now by his reaction to her. All right, she'd made love with him against his will, but was that all he had to say? *Thanks?* God, she wanted some evidence of his commitment. Despite her best intentions, it hadn't been an emotionless thing to her. 'Um— where are you going?'

'Back to London?' he suggested, turning to her and buckling his belt, and she was instantly conscious of every flaw in her own body. She twisted round and rolled onto her stomach, feeling more comfortable in that position. 'I left my car parked on the village green.'

Fliss expelled a trembling breath. 'Don't you want to talk?'

Morgan's nostrils flared. 'What about?'

Fliss swallowed. 'Well—how about telling me what that scar is on your thigh?'

'Oh, that.' Morgan heaved a sigh. 'It's nothing to be proud of.'

'Nevertheless...'

'Nevertheless, now that you've proved I'm whole again, you want your pound of flesh,' he muttered harshly, and she thought how unfair that was in the circumstances.

'I just think I have a right to know,' she said tensely. 'Did they do that when they captured you? I thought you said they only shot your driver.'

'They did.'

Morgan reached for his shirt and jacket from the bed, his lips twisting as she flinched away from his hand. He wasn't to know that her reaction was anything but rejection. For a heart-stopping moment she'd thought he'd changed his mind.

Now, after buttoning his shirt, he slipped on his jacket and ran a weary hand over his hair. 'I thought I had a foolproof plan for getting away from the camp,' he said at last. 'I stole one of the jeeps and was hightailing it down the mountain when one of Ungave's patrols opened fire.'

'One of Ungave's patrols!' Fliss was horrified. 'But I thought you said you hadn't tried to escape.'

'I said I wasn't a hero,' he corrected her drily. 'The patrol left me for dead, but luckily Julius's men found me before I bled to death.'

Fliss caught her breath. 'Oh, Morgan...'

'Don't,' he advised her grimly. 'Don't go getting all emotional about me now. I was a fool; I realise that, but one of the bullets was too bloody close for comfort. I—had an infection afterwards. The camp doctor seemed to think it might create a problem. Right then, I wasn't too concerned. I was just glad to be alive.'

'And that's why—'

'Do I have to spell it out for you?' He picked up his overcoat and turned away. 'Yeah, that's why I haven't been with a woman since. But thanks to you my problems are over, aren't they? Aren't I lucky having a wife who's so considerate she'd—have sex with her soon-to-be ex-husband rather than let him suffer?'

It might have been an apology, but the sarcasm in his voice tore her apart. 'That's a—cruel way of putting it,' she said, sucking in her breath defensively.

'Well, it wasn't exactly a *kind* thing to do,' he retorted, without a trace of sympathy in his voice. 'Thanks—but you should have saved yourself for Graham,' he added bitterly. 'I bet the poor bastard doesn't know how desperate for sex you are!'

CHAPTER TWELVE

MORGAN regretted renting the apartment in Salisbury now.

When he'd first thought about finding accommodation in the Whittersley area, it had been with the idea of making life difficult for Fliss. Despite his apparent acceptance of her relationship with Graham Bland, he was still very bitter, and it was only when he'd discovered the problems she'd had to cope with that he'd begun to realise that it hadn't all been her fault.

But it had been hard, damned hard, coming to terms with the fact that his wife had fallen in love with someone else. When he'd met the man himself it had taken every scrap of self-control he had to treat him civilly. God, he'd wanted to flatten his smug face and he could have, too, despite all his mother's fretting about him conserving his strength.

He'd sensed that Bland was apprehensive of him. Not afraid, exactly, but anxious about what he might do. The poor devil had probably been more concerned about his social standing than any actual physical damage he might do to him, but Morgan had known that Fliss would never forgive him if he attacked the other man.

And, although it was stupid, he knew, he'd wanted to remain on civil terms with her. That was why, when his parents had loaned him money to be paid back when his next advance came through he'd rented the apartment in Salisbury, because it would have enabled him to keep in touch with her. There was no satisfaction to be gained in cutting off all communication with her. He'd had some crazy idea about making her regret what had happened, maybe even making her jealous, and he couldn't do that if she didn't even know he was alive.

His lips twisted. If he was alive! It was because she hadn't known he was alive that he'd lost his wife in the first place. If only Julius had let him get in touch with her; if only he'd trusted him that much. But Julius had suffered too much in his life because he and his family had trusted other people. Even members of his own family, Morgan remembered ruefully. When Julius's uncle had been deposed by General Ungave—when he'd been *executed*, he amended harshly—his aunt had negotiated a place in the new government for her own son by betraying her in-laws.

Not that that helped Morgan now. As he walked around the spacious rooms of the converted Victorian town house, with its much vaunted view of the cathedral, he realised that once again Fliss had confounded him. He'd gone to the cottage that afternoon in a spirit of conciliation, but instead of making his peace with her he had allowed her to destroy what little self-respect he had left.

He groaned. Why had she done it? Why had she shown him what might have been, only to take it away from him again? He didn't really believe that it was because she was so desperate for a man to make love to her, although he'd have sworn that Bland had never touched her. A naïve belief perhaps, but she'd had an untouched quality, despite her efforts to appear at ease with her sex. He'd have said that she'd been as nervous as he was, but with less reason.

He scowled at the view. It was possible that Graham had never touched her, he supposed. Or was that just wishful thinking? From what his mother had said, he'd gained the impression that the Reverend Graham Bland was a fairly old-fashioned type of clergyman. Stuffy, she'd said, with a grimace of distaste, when he'd told his parents that he and Fliss were separating, but he found he liked that description better now. Whatever happened in the future, it was a small consolation to know that Fliss hadn't betrayed him in the past.

Even so, everything had changed. The idea of bringing

her here, of showing her this comfortably furnished first-floor apartment, no longer held any attraction. He didn't want her here. He didn't want to have to live with her image haunting his every waking moment as well as every sleeping one. Besides, how could he be sure he wouldn't give in to the urge to touch her again? So long as he'd believed himself immune from temptation—or, at least, a martyr to it—there'd been some merit in showing her what she'd lost. But now all he could think about was what he'd lost, and the need to leave this place, to put as many miles between himself and Fliss as was humanly possible, seemed the only sane thing to do.

And yet...

And yet...

He exhaled, and turned to rest his hips on the wide windowsill behind him. How could he do it? How could he abandon any hope of seeing her again? Of *being with* her again? Whatever commitment she'd made to Bland, was he really prepared to give her up without a fight?

But she didn't want him, a small voice mocked insistently. Her only reason for letting him near her was to prove to him—and herself—that his fears of impotence were groundless. She hadn't wanted him on her conscience, so she'd done what was necessary to remove the guilt. And in so doing she had robbed him of his only hold on her affections.

So what was he going to do? He'd had the best part of two weeks to consider his options, but he was still no closer to a decision than he had ever been. He seemed to be in a kind of limbo, with no obvious escape in view. Had he lived four years waiting for this moment only to lose it now because he couldn't face a possible defeat?

When he'd left the cottage and driven back to London, he'd been too stunned by what had happened to consider the future. In consequence, the lease he'd already taken on this apartment had gone ahead as planned. It wasn't until the estate agency had contacted him, informing him that the keys were waiting for collection, that he'd been forced to face the results of his own foolishness. Any revenge he'd planned seemed futile now. So why couldn't he just get on with his life and allow Fliss to get on with hers?

Because he still loved her.

Anger gripped him. Pushing himself up from the sill, he walked across the carpeted floor to the marble fireplace and plucked the letter he'd dropped there from the mantel. It had a Nyandan postmark and it had arrived at his London address along with the letter from the Salisbury estate agents. It was from Julius, and was embossed with the seal of the new President of the Nyandan Republic, and Paul Giles, who handed the letter to him at the breakfast table, had been suitably impressed by its official status.

'Friends in high places,' he'd remarked, winking at his wife, and Morgan had given him a wry look. 'Well—' Paul had looked slightly embarrassed then '—thank heavens you knew the guy. At least you're still alive, which is more than can be said for some of the poor bastards who were caught up in the fighting.'

'Yes.' Morgan had smoothed the letter between his fingers without opening it. He'd fixed the other man with a steady gaze. 'But you didn't know that when you sent me out there. You said it was safe. You said President Ungave had the whole situation under his control.'

'I thought he did.' Paul had cast his wife a rueful look. 'I said as much to you, didn't I, Lindy? I said the contract was a piece of cake.'

'I'm sure you thought it was,' his wife had murmured loyally, but Morgan, who knew Linda Giles of old, was aware that she'd say anything if it suited her own purposes. She had never forgiven Morgan for snubbing her advances at an office party many years ago, and she regarded him now with barely concealed contempt.

'Well, it turned out all right in the end,' Paul had added

swiftly. 'I mean, you're here, aren't you? And it's obvious that Mdola views you very highly.'

'My wife doesn't,' Morgan had remarked drily, slitting the flap of the envelope with his finger, and Linda Giles had given him a curious stare.

'She doesn't?' she'd asked in surprise, and Morgan had realised he had made a tactical mistake. 'But I thought that was why you were getting an apartment in Salisbury. So that Fliss could keep her job in—whatever that place is called.'

'Whittersley,' Morgan had said patiently. 'It's called Whittersley. And, no. The apartment's for me, not for her.'

'Really?'

Morgan could practically see the speculation in her eyes, and, berating himself for saying so much, he'd pulled the letter from its sheath.

It was a typewritten missive, but signed in Julius's distinctive scrawl, on paper that was suitably thick and expensive. Morgan suspected that aspect of it was more Ungave's choice than Mdola's, but standards had to be upheld.

After the usual pleasantries in which Julius expressed the hope that his friend was now fully restored to health, he turned to more official matters. His formal investiture was to be held at the end of the year, as part of the millennium celebrations, and he hoped that Morgan and his wife would be able to attend. He wanted to take the opportunity to thank the other man for his help in defeating Ungave's forces, but mainly he wanted to renew his acquaintance with him, to meet his wife, and to present him with an honorary award.

It was the kind of letter that anyone would be proud to receive. Morgan knew there had been speculation in the press that he was to be honored in this way, but this was official and he remembered wishing he could have shown it to Fliss. Would she have been proud, he wondered, or would she have seen it as confirmation of what she already suspected: that he could have got in touch with her if he'd really tried?

He didn't know. He didn't honestly know what she would have thought, and he was unlikely to find out. He couldn't go and ask her. He'd embarrassed himself too many times already, and there was a limit to how much humiliation he could take.

Which left him with the same dilemma, he reflected, returning the envelope to the mantelpiece. He had to make a decision about the apartment before he could make a real effort to put the past behind him. But would living here, only a stone's throw from Whittersley, be the most sensible thing to do? Fliss probably did her shopping in Salisbury. He could run into her at any time, and while she could probably live with that, could he? Could he bear the thought of her marrying Bland and maybe having his child? What if he saw her pushing a pram?

The buzz of the intercom interrupted his painful musings, and almost gratefully he moved to pick up the receiver. He couldn't imagine that anyone but the estate agent who had handled the lease he'd taken on the apartment knew where he lived, and his response was suitably flat. 'Yes?'

'Morgan?' It was a female voice and for a moment his heart leapt. But then she spoke again. 'It's me—Linda. Can I come up?'

Fliss knelt at the back of the church. It was an attractive church, with a carved choir screen and an impressive stained-glass window above the altar. There were scarlet cushions in all the pews and Graham's army of helpers made sure there were always huge urns of flowers occupying every vacant space. At present, with the approach of Easter, there were no flowers on the altar, but it was warmed by the light of the candles flickering in their sconces at either end of the damask-covered table.

Graham was kneeling at the altar, and she guessed he didn't realise she was still there. The mid-week communion service was over, and the rest of the small congregation had already left. This service, held mainly for people who couldn't make the Sunday service, was never very heavily attended, and no one had paid any attention to Fliss still kneeling in her pew.

She wouldn't have been there herself had she not felt the need to speak to Graham, and she knew when she'd asked Mrs Buxton for the day off that the headmistress had assumed she was going to spend the time with her husband. But what she had to say to Graham couldn't wait any longer, and she preferred to get it over in daylight rather than invite him to the cottage after dark.

Graham got to his feet at last, and Fliss, whose knees had been growing increasingly numb, eased herself gratefully onto the bench seat. Surely he was almost ready to leave? she mused hopefully. He never used to spend so long at the altar, and she could only assume he was still making atonement for what he saw as his own weakness.

Which should have made what she had to say to him easier. But it didn't. On the contrary, she was uncomfortably aware that the reason he spent so long in the church these days was that he couldn't dismiss his feelings for her. Of late, he'd been finding more and more excuses to come to the cottage in the evenings. It was as if he thought that as she and Morgan had separated he didn't have to be so circumspect of his own actions any more.

But Fliss knew she couldn't allow it to go on. Somehow she had to explain to him that Morgan's coming back had changed everything. Not just how she felt about him, although that was relevant, too. But the way she viewed the future, and her own participation in it.

Goodness knew, she'd tried to have this conversation with him before today. Twice, when he'd appeared at the cottage, ostensibly to deliver some message from the committee about her contribution to the church's activities, she'd attempted to tell him how she felt. But, as if he'd sensed what was coming, Graham had always sidestepped any personal exchange between them, and she was left with the feeling that he didn't want to know.

It wasn't his fault, she acknowledged. And there was a certain irony in the way she felt now. When she'd believed Morgan was dead, she'd had no doubt about her feelings for Graham. He was a kind and thoughtful man—a decent man, as she'd told Morgan—and any woman would be proud to know he cared about her.

But her feelings had changed; she'd changed. Where once security and safety in a relationship had seemed desirable, now she doubted her own ability to be satisfied with anything less than what she and Morgan had shared. Graham was secure, and safe, but she wasn't in love with him. She loved him still; of course she did. But loving wasn't enough.

She realised that her attraction to Graham had been formed by the very emotions that were driving her away from him now. She'd always known, subconsciously perhaps, that she could never duplicate what she'd had with Morgan, so she'd turned to a man who was his exact opposite. And that had worked very well, so long as she'd believed Morgan was dead and gone. His return had exploded that particular myth, and it wasn't fair—to either her or Graham—to try and sustain a lie.

She sighed. She hoped he'd understand; that he wouldn't be too hurt by the decision she'd had to make. But seeing Morgan again had delivered a crippling blow to the foundations of her relationship with Graham, and when they'd made love... Her breath caught in her throat. That was when she'd realised exactly what she was giving up.

Not that Morgan had shared her feelings, she admitted sadly, watching as Graham doused the candles on the altar. She hoped Graham would believe her when she told him that Morgan wasn't to blame for her decision. She cringed every time she remembered the way that she'd behaved.

God, what a pathetic creature he must have thought she was. He'd totally misunderstood her motives, and that was hard to forgive. Did he really think she could have given herself to him without her emotions being involved? Had she ever stopped loving him? she wondered now. Or had she simply buried the pain so deep that only the consummation of her love had been capable of tearing away the layers of self-deceit?

Graham was stepping back from the altar at last, taking some time to ensure that he hadn't forgotten anything before backing down the steps and crossing himself one last time. Where once his attention to ceremonial detail had pleased her, now Fliss found herself getting impatient at his slowness, and she closed her eyes, again, trying to regain some measure of inner tranquillity.

'Fliss?' His voice disturbed her, and she opened her eyes to find him standing at the end of the pew. 'Why aren't you in school?'

'I'm playing truant,' said Fliss lightly, trying not to resent the accusatory tone in his voice. She wasn't a small girl, for heaven's sake. 'I was hoping we could talk. Are you ready to go?'

'Not quite.' Graham looked up the aisle towards the vestry. 'I've got one or two odds and ends to attend to first.'

'Then I'll wait.'

'No.' Graham evidently didn't want her here where their being together might cause gossip. 'That is—couldn't I just call round this evening?'

'I'd prefer it to be this morning,' said Fliss doggedly. She hesitated. 'I hoped you might walk me home.'

'Well, I can't.' Graham's voice had taken on an irritable tone. 'Fliss, I'm sure this can wait.' His eyes darkened. 'Is it about Riker? What has he been saying now?'

'It's not about Morgan,' said Fliss defensively, but she knew it was. 'Look, it won't take long. Can't I wait?'

'I'd rather you didn't.' Graham sighed. 'You're not ill, are you? That's not why you're taking time off school?'

'I'm fine.' Fliss tried to be patient. 'Mrs Buxton has given me the day off. Look—let's compromise, shall we? You can come and have coffee at the cottage before you go home.'

'Oh—all right.'

He wasn't enthusiastic, but Fliss was too relieved to worry about that. Besides, she was thinking seriously of leaving Whittersley at the end of the summer term, so any anxieties he had about his reputation would soon be removed.

She was carrying the tray into the living room when Graham knocked at the door. He came in, shedding his cape, and she was glad to see he'd taken her at her word. Usually he went home to change before visiting the cottage, but as he was still wearing his cassock she guessed he'd acceded to her need for punctuality.

'This looks nice,' he said, bending to take a biscuit from the tray. 'Mmm, ginger. My favourite!'

'Why don't you sit down and I'll go and get the coffee?' suggested Fliss, wishing he weren't watching her quite so closely. 'I won't be a minute.'

But when she came back it was to find that he was still standing on the hearth, and she realised with a sense of unease that he'd finally detected that something was wrong.

'What is it?' he asked as she set the pot on the low table. 'I get the feeling that something's upset you.'

'It has.' Fliss decided there was no point in pretending otherwise. 'Oh, Graham, why don't you sit down? I'm sure we'd both feel better if we relaxed.'

Graham still didn't move, and because she couldn't prevaricate any longer Fliss plunged into words. 'I don't think

I can marry you, Graham,' she said, avoiding any mention of her husband. 'I—well, I'm sorry. But I can't.'

'Why not?'

'Why not?' His response shouldn't have surprised her, but it did. He must have had an inkling of how she was feeling. 'I just can't go through with it, I'm afraid.'

'Riker won't give you a divorce, is that it?'

'No, that's not it.' Fliss gazed at him in dismay. 'Morgan has nothing to do with my decision. I haven't seen him for weeks as you very well know.'

'Haven't you?' Graham regarded her rather sceptically. 'So you're telling me this decision to call off our relationship has nothing to do with him?'

'Only indirectly,' said Fliss unhappily. 'I just don't think we're—compatible, after all.'

'And what have I done to put this doubt into your mind?' he demanded. 'Just a couple of days ago you agreed to help me at the May fair.'

'And I will.' Fliss shook her head. 'This is not something I'm proud of, Graham, believe me. You've always been there for me when I needed you, and I'll never forget that.'

'But your husband's return does have something to do with this, doesn't it?' He spoke harshly. 'Credit me with some intelligence, Fliss, please. You had no doubts about us, no doubts about us being together until Riker came back from the dead!'

'But that was because I thought he was dead,' protested Fliss unhappily, feeling guilty. 'Try to understand, I never thought I'd see him again.'

'But now you have, and you want him back again, is that it? Or has he been making threats that I don't know anything about?'

'Of course not.' Fliss was appalled. 'Morgan's not like that. He's never threatened a woman in his life.'

'I doubt you know what he's really like,' retorted

Graham shortly. 'In my opinion, he'd do anything to break us up.'

'Do you think so?' Fliss spoke rather wistfully now, but then, realising what she was saying, she hurried to make amends. 'It's not Morgan's fault,' she insisted. 'It's mine. Ever since he came back—'

'You've felt guilty; I know,' Graham sighed. 'Oh, my dear, I do know how you feel, believe me. I've been struggling with my conscience, too. But I'm sure you need have no doubts about your husband's well-being. Men like him are never short of women. I should know.'

Fliss frowned. 'How should you know?'

'Oh—' Graham raised a hand now. 'I have had some experience in these matters,' he said, his ears turning pink. 'You'll see, there'll be no problem about getting a divorce.'

Fliss exhaled wearily. 'You don't understand, Graham.'

'What don't I understand?'

'I—I don't want a divorce.' She flushed now, and pressed the heels of her hands together. 'I mean it—whether I see Morgan again or not.'

'I don't believe it.' He stared incredulously at her.

'It's true.' She felt the tears prick her eyes. 'I'm sorry, Graham, truly I am, but I love him. I think I always have. I just lost sight of it for a while.'

Graham made a strangled sound. 'You can't be serious!'

'I'm afraid I am.'

'But you say you have no guarantee that Riker wants to—to renew your relationship.'

'I know that.'

'Then—'

'Whatever happens, I can't marry you,' said Fliss bleakly. 'And I couldn't let you go on thinking that I might. I am sorry, Graham. I never wanted to hurt you in this way.'

Graham blinked. 'Are you sure Riker hasn't been in touch with you?'

'Of course I'm sure.'

'Because I don't believe you've thought this through. We're not children, Fliss; we're adults. We know there's no real happiness for any of us. Not in this life, anyway. We just look for security and contentment, and if there's also an element of sexual attraction there so much the better.'

Fliss was appalled. 'That's not true.'

'Of course it's true.' Graham was a little belligerent now, and she hoped he wasn't going to create a scene. 'We suit one another, Fliss. We are compatible. For heaven's sake, you've still got my ring.'

The ring! Fliss had forgotten about that, but Graham would be practical to the last. Perhaps he thought she wanted to keep it. He didn't know her very well if he thought that.

'I'm sorry,' she said again. 'I'm sorry you feel that way. I really hoped that you'd understand how I feel.'

Graham's face was getting red now, and he ran his finger around the inside of his collar as he always did when he was feeling hot. But, although she'd usually found his action quite endearing, now she sensed a certain menace in his stare.

'I think you must have taken leave of your senses,' he said at last, and she hoped that was all he was going to say.

'Please forgive me,' she murmured. And then, with feeling, 'I'm hoping that we can still be friends.'

'Friends!' Graham took an angry breath. 'Friends!' He shook his head. 'I don't think you've given a thought to my feelings at all. All you're thinking about is your own happiness, and no one else's. How am I going to face my parishioners after this?'

Fliss swallowed. 'But they know—'

'What do they know?'

'Well, that you and I have split up, of course. That since Morgan's come back—'

'They also know that you and your husband are not living together,' pointed out Graham sharply. 'I know they all expect us to make an announcement fairly soon.'

'Oh, Graham, that's not true.' She bit her lip. 'And does it matter what anyone says? This is our affair. Can't we keep it to ourselves?'

'So you say.' He snorted. 'But I'm a public figure, Fliss. I have an image to uphold. People understood our situation before. But now they're going to say, Poor old Bland. He can't keep a woman; he's been left at the altar again.'

Fliss stared at him. 'Again?'

'Yes, again.' He scowled now, as if realising he'd said more than he'd intended. 'I was—engaged before.'

'When?'

'Does it matter?'

Fliss swallowed. 'It does to me.'

'Well—it was before you came to the village. Just before, actually. She was also a widow—a real one, this time.' His lips curled. 'Did no one tell you?'

'No.' Fliss was surprised. He'd never mentioned another woman to her. On the contrary, he'd made a point of stating that she was the only woman he'd ever loved. 'What happened?'

'She left me.' Graham was bitter. 'For another man. I believe she said she loved him, too. Although it's my belief it was his money she was after.'

'Oh, Graham.'

'So now you know,' he declared brusquely. 'And now you think you can make a fool of me as well.'

CHAPTER THIRTEEN

FLISS groaned now. 'Graham, I don't want to make a fool of you. I care about you.'

'Do you?' He turned to her then, grasping her shoulders so that she was forced to look into his flushed face. 'And I care about you. That's what I'm trying to tell you.' He frowned. 'Is it because I've not been a very—demonstrative lover?'

'No.' Fliss was alarmed at this unexpected turn of events. She twisted away, trying not to appear too dismayed that he should think such a thing. 'Look—we'll talk about this again, when you've got more time.' She swallowed. 'I'll get your ring.'

It was a relief to run upstairs, to expunge some of the adrenalin that was pulsing through her veins. The atmosphere downstairs had suddenly become oppressive. She would never have believed that Graham could behave so aggressively. But then, she'd never had to confront this side of his character before.

She was rummaging in the drawer of the bedside table, searching frantically for the ring which she knew she'd put there when she'd first learned that Morgan was alive, when she heard the stairs creak behind her. She froze, hardly daring to believe what she was hearing, but then Graham appeared in the doorway, a sombre figure in his black cassock and thick-soled shoes.

'So this is your bedroom,' he said, seemingly unaware of any impropriety, and she stared at him with anxious eyes.

'Graham, what are you—?'

'I've often wondered what your bedroom was like,' he

continued, stepping into the room and surveying its appointments with disturbingly intense eyes. 'It's very nice. Very—feminine.'

Fliss couldn't speak. She didn't even want to consider what had brought him upstairs, and her fingers scrabbled urgently for the ring. She couldn't help remembering what had happened when Morgan had followed her upstairs, but despite her anger at her husband she'd never felt afraid of him.

Was she afraid of Graham?

The truth was, she didn't know. She wouldn't have said so before, but suddenly he seemed a stranger to her, and she thought how odd it was that she'd never suspected he might have a darker side.

Her fingers closed on the ring at that moment and, with a cry of relief, she pulled it out of the drawer. 'Here it is,' she said, making a determined effort to behave as if Graham's being in her bedroom was perfectly normal. 'I'm sorry it's taken so long to find.'

'That's all right.' He was terrifyingly casual. 'I'm in no hurry.' His thick soles covered the carpet to the windows. 'Oh, yes. What a pleasant view.'

Fliss could feel beads of perspiration breaking out all over her. Although she was only wearing a sleeveless waistcoat over a shirt and leggings, she felt uncomfortably hot. The fingers gripping his ring were slippery with sweat. What was he doing here? Why had he followed her upstairs?

'Graham...' She didn't know what to say and he turned to look at her with unexpectedly pitying eyes. 'Graham, please; we can't talk here. Let's go downstairs and have some coffee.' She paused. 'It'll be getting cold.'

'He's got another woman, you know.'

Fliss was trying to edge him towards the door when his startling announcement arrested her. 'What did you say?'

'I said, I believe your husband's got another woman,'

declared Graham, heaving a sigh. 'I'm sorry, Fliss. I didn't want to tell you. I hoped I wouldn't have to tell you. But you've left me no choice.'

Fliss felt as if all the strength had gone out of her. 'Morgan's seeing someone else?' she breathed unsteadily. 'I—I don't believe it.'

'It's true.' Graham tried to take her hands in his but she thrust them behind her back, and his lips tightened. 'I saw him with her myself.'

Fliss felt sick. 'Where? When?' Her stomach was churning. 'Why didn't you tell me?'

'I am telling you,' he reminded her quietly. And then, as if realising some further explanation was necessary, he added, 'I went to see him, you see. Or rather, I tried to. Yes. After meeting him that afternoon, I inadvertently found out where he was living.'

Fliss sank weakly down onto the side of the bed, all thought about the impropriety of Graham's behaviour giving way to a stunned feeling of betrayal. Morgan was seeing another woman, she thought incredulously. Dear God, she'd never have believed it could be as painful as this.

'You didn't know?' Graham ventured now, and she looked up at him with haggard eyes.

'No, I didn't know,' she said tightly, wondering if he was enjoying this. She sniffed. 'How did you find out?'

'I told you, I went to his apartment,' said Graham patiently, and Fliss knew a sudden sense of relief.

'Then you're wrong,' she cried, almost dizzily. 'The woman you saw, she's not Morgan's girlfriend, she's Paul's wife.'

'Paul?' Graham looked confused now. 'Who is Paul? There's only Riker's name on the plate outside the door.'

Fliss got shakily to her feet again. 'You mean in London, don't you?'

'Not London, no. Salisbury.' Graham adjusted the belt

of his cassock. 'Riker's living in Salisbury. Didn't he tell you?'

Fliss could hardly speak. 'Morgan's living in Salisbury?' she choked. 'But how did you know?'

'Well, I happened to see him in town,' admitted Graham, not a little ruefully. 'He didn't see me, of course, but I couldn't help wondering what he was doing there.'

'So what?' Fliss frowned. 'Are you saying you followed him?'

Graham shifted a little uncomfortably. 'Well, yes. I was curious as to why he should be in Salisbury, I suppose. Then when he seemed familiar with the place, I got intrigued.'

Fliss shook her head. 'And you saw him with this woman?'

'No, not then.' Graham paced about the bedroom. 'He was alone, as I said. He turned onto Cloister Park. Er, that's the name of the terrace of houses where he's rented an apartment. After he'd gone inside, I took a look.'

Fliss was devastated. She couldn't believe that Morgan had rented an apartment in Salisbury without telling her. Why would he do such a thing? What reason could he have? Was he planning to parade a string of mistresses in front of her?

'So—so when—?' she began tremulously, and although she couldn't continue Graham seemed to comprehend what she meant.

'Some time later,' he said gently. 'Knowing he was living there, just a few miles from Whittersley, I felt I had to know what his intentions towards you were. But when I arrived at Cloister Park I saw this young woman ringing the bell of your husband's apartment, and I waited in the car until I saw him let her in.'

Fliss felt as if someone had just driven a knife into her stomach. Until then, until Graham had actually explained how he'd got his information, she'd hoped there might have been some mistake. But, as far as she was aware, Morgan knew no one else in this area, and if this woman knew where he lived she had to be a friend.

Which meant she must have come down from London to see him. Perhaps she'd driven down with Morgan and he'd kept that piece of information from her, too. What price now her pitiful attempt to show him he wasn't impotent? He must have been laughing at her efforts. He'd probably known it wasn't true all along.

'I'm sorry, Fliss…'

Graham had stopped his pacing and come to stand in front of her now, and, looking up into his indulgent face, Fliss wanted to scream. Was this why Graham was here, in her bedroom? she wondered bitterly. Because he believed she'd be grateful for his support?

'I think you'd better go, Graham,' she told him stiffly, realising that nothing he did now could hurt her as much. She felt numb, yet every nerve in her body was jumping. She just wanted to be alone to lick her wounds in private.

'Are you sure?'

Graham put his fingers beneath her chin and tipped her face up to his and it was all she could do not to dash his hand away. 'I'm sure,' she said, through clenched teeth, but although he must have sensed her withdrawal he didn't move away.

'I know this has probably been a shock,' he went on evenly, choosing his words with care, 'but isn't it really for the best—?'

'The best?' Fliss did grab his hand then, thrusting the ring that was still sweaty from her fingers into it. 'The best for whom?' she demanded wildly. 'Not for me.' She shook her head so vigorously that the cord on her braid flew off and her heavy hair spilled about her shoulders. 'Never for me!'

'Fliss!' Graham's patience seemed to be wearing thin. 'Fliss, I don't think you realise what you're saying.'

'Don't I?' She was indignant. 'And I suppose you didn't know exactly what you were doing when you came here?'

'You invited me here,' protested Graham angrily. 'For heaven's sake, Fliss, I didn't want to hurt you.'

'But you have,' she said painfully. 'You said you didn't want to tell me, but you did. Why? It wasn't for my benefit, was it? It was for yours, Graham, just for yours.'

'Fliss!' Graham looked hurt now, and she knew a moment's remorse for making him the scapegoat for her own misery. 'How can you say such things?'

Fliss's shoulders sagged. As suddenly as it had appeared all the aggression she had been feeling towards him disappeared. In its place was a desperate feeling of her own isolation, and, tipping her head back on her shoulders, she gave a weary sigh.

'I'm sorry,' she said, pushing her hair back behind her ears. 'I shouldn't have said that. Forgive me.'

'Of course.'

Graham sounded as if he meant it, and she wondered how she could ever have doubted his integrity. He had always been there for her, hadn't he? In good times and bad. And she had had no reason to blame him for Morgan's indiscretions.

But when she would have gone towards the door Graham moved to block her path. 'Not yet,' he said, a little thickly, and before she could guess his intentions he'd slipped his arms around her waist and pressed his lips to hers.

Her astonishment was total. All the fears he'd evoked in her earlier came back, and she recognised how foolish she'd been to dismiss his uncharacteristic behaviour. But somehow the things he'd told her had been of such a private nature that she'd persuaded herself that that was the real reason he'd come upstairs.

But she'd been wrong; just as she'd been wrong about so many things, she thought unhappily. Had he been planning this all along? Had he just been softening her up by telling her about Morgan? Had he hoped she'd be so dis-illusioned with her husband that whatever he chose to do she wouldn't turn him down?

His mouth was hot, hot and wet, his tongue forcing its way into her mouth with no sensitivity whatsoever. She was doubly shocked because Graham had always been so gentle with her before, and her spirits sank at this evidence of his lack of respect for her.

'No—' she choked, when she could get her mouth free of him, but she doubted he could hear her. He was too intent on pulling the hem of her shirt out of the waistband of her leggings, pressing his face into her neck and biting the soft lobe of her ear.

Her flesh cringed. She was repulsed, but there was little she could do to stop him. He was so big, so powerfully built, all those stodgy meals combining to make a solid whole. In addition to which, he was stronger than she was, and he'd come at her so forcefully, she'd almost been swept off her feet.

'For pity's sake, Graham,' she cried as his efforts to take her shirt off caused several of the buttons to go skittering across the floor. She was endeavouring not to panic, but it wasn't easy. His violence was making her feel ill.

'Ah, Fliss, Fliss,' he crooned as his groping fingers found her breasts. 'You've no idea how long I've wanted to do this. I'll make you forget any man who's ever loved you before me.'

'This—is—not—love,' she protested jerkily, trying hopelessly to push his hands away. She felt a sense of dis-belief, a sense of violation. How could he do this? Had he completely lost his mind?

The side of the bed batted the backs of her legs and she realised that had been his intention. He'd been propelling her in this direction from the start. He'd let her back away from him because it had suited his purpose. If she recoiled from him again, they'd be on the bed.

In the event, she didn't have to do anything. He simply
leaned his weight against her and she had no choice but to
tumble back onto the mattress. As it was, his weight nearly
knocked all the breath out of her, and she lay there panting
helplessly as he studied her face.

'You're so beautiful,' he said, sliding one hand into her
hair, and she closed her eyes against his avid stare.

'How beautiful?' she demanded bitterly. 'More beautiful
than your calling? The bishop's going to be so disappointed
in you when he hears about this.'

Graham groaned then. It was a harsh, animalistic sound,
and Fliss waited despairingly for what was to come. She
hadn't done herself any favours by taunting him, she
thought bleakly. She'd just made him more determined, that
was all.

The sudden lift of the mattress as Graham's weight was
removed startled her. Her eyes flew open to find him on
his feet straightening the folds of his cassock beside the
bed. 'Dear heaven,' he was mumbling frantically, 'what
must you be thinking of me?' His eyes turned guiltily towards her. 'I'm so sorry, Fliss. I've never done anything
like this before.'

Fliss was trembling so badly she could hardly speak, but
her hands moved automatically to draw together the gaping
sides of her shirt. She swung her feet to the floor, and
scrambled off the bed as soon as he moved away from it.
She was terrified he might change his mind.

'You will forgive me, won't you?'

He was imploring her now, but although he held his
hands out towards her she didn't make the mistake of
touching him again. The ring was lying on the floor, and,
picking it up, Fliss laid it on the chest of drawers beside
him. 'Just take your ring and go,' she managed tremulously.
She couldn't wait for him to leave so that she could go and
scrub herself clean.

'You won't—that is—you know I had the best of intentions, don't you?' he stammered. 'I love you, Fliss. I'd never hurt you for the world.' He licked his lips. 'But—you're right, the bishop might not understand my motives. I'm afraid he's a little old-fashioned when it comes to—to sex.'

'If you're afraid I might report you to the bishop, then forget it,' said Fliss unsteadily. 'But if you ever—ever do anything like this again—'

'I won't.' Graham's hands dropped to his sides, and he shook his head defeatedly. 'I just can't believe you'd prefer a man like Riker to me.'

Fliss's lips tightened. She wasn't prepared to get into that. She wasn't prepared to discuss her private affairs with him ever again. So far as she was concerned, Graham had destroyed not just her hopes but any chance of retaining her friendship. It seemed as if she was destined to give her trust to men who didn't deserve it.

She followed him down the stairs, waiting with barely concealed impatience for him to don his cape and move towards the door. She could have allowed him to let himself out, but she wanted to lock the door behind him. She wouldn't feel secure until he was safely out of the cottage.

'Will I see you at church on Sunday?' he asked, pausing on the threshold, and she had to steel herself not to push him down the steps.

'Perhaps,' she said, but there was little optimism in her expression. 'Goodbye, Graham,' she added, and carefully closed the door.

She didn't care if he heard her employ the deadlock. She couldn't forget that he still had a key to the cottage, and there was no way she could risk him invading her territory again. The man whom she'd turned to, the man she'd trusted, had almost raped her. If he hadn't been so afraid of what the bishop might say, she'd never have fought him off.

Her shoulders sagged. Dear God, she thought, what was

she going to do now? She realised she'd pinned her hopes on seeing Morgan again. But if he'd found someone else there was no chance of going back...

Fliss was marking a pile of exercise books when she heard someone at the door.

It was quite late in the evening, almost a quarter to ten, in fact, and her skin prickled alarmingly at the sound. She was sure it could only be Graham, come to make another bid for her forgiveness; or perhaps to threaten her with eviction if she didn't obey his demands.

The knock came again and, realising she couldn't ignore it, however much she'd like to, Fliss got unwillingly up from her chair. If it was Graham, she didn't think he'd risk a scene that might be overheard by any of his parishioners. And if he had come to apologise again she didn't have to open the door.

Realising she could find out who it was by looking out of the bay window, she crossed the room and pulled the curtain aside. It wasn't Graham, she saw with some relief; it was Morgan. She dropped the curtain. For heaven's sake, what did he want at this time of night?

Deciding the likelihood of two men trying to attack her in one day was very doubtful, she squared her shoulders and walked out into the hall. Whatever he wanted, she wasn't afraid of Morgan. Well, afraid that he might find out how she really felt about him perhaps.

She opened the door. 'Morgan,' she said, hoping her voice didn't sound as nervous to him as it did to her. 'What a surprise!'

'Can I come in?'

It was a cool evening, and although he was wearing the dark overcoat he'd worn the last time he was here his face looked pale.

'Why not?' she said, stepping back and allowing him

entry. 'Although I have to say I didn't think you'd want to come here again.'

Morgan gave her a hard look as he passed her, but Fliss tried not to be intimidated by his stare. She closed the door and set the lock, telling herself that she was only thinking of security, and then followed him into the lamplit living room with an anxious heart.

'I gather you're surprised to see me,' he remarked, from his usual stance in the middle of the floor. 'Are you busy? Am I interrupting you? I suppose you think I should have waited until tomorrow.'

Fliss shrugged, linking her hands at her waist and wishing she'd put something respectable on after her bath. But the shirt and leggings she'd been wearing earlier had gone into the dustbin, and her shabby sweats and one of Morgan's old shirts had definitely seen better days.

Her hair was loose, too. She'd washed it to get the smell of Graham's fingers out of it, and then, after towelling it dry, had left it free about her shoulders. She pushed it back now, aware that she probably looked like a witch. She wasn't wearing any make-up, and she knew she, too, looked pale.

'I had a visitor this evening,' Morgan stated at last, when it became obvious that Fliss had nothing to say. 'That's why it's so late now. But I had to know if what he said was right.'

Fliss's mouth went dry. 'What *he* said?' she echoed faintly. 'Who—who's *he*?'

'Can't you guess?' Morgan was sardonic. 'It was Bland, of course. He'd apparently been waiting to see me for some time. But I went up to London this morning and I didn't get back until about seven, I suppose.'

Fliss couldn't believe it. 'Graham went to see you?' she echoed faintly. And then, more apprehensively, she asked, 'What did he want?'

'This and that.' Morgan was watching her closely. 'I

thought you might have sent him, as a matter of fact.' His lips twisted. 'But I can tell from your expression that I was wrong.'

Fliss shook her head. 'You—you thought *I* might have sent him?' she said, her voice barely audible. She licked her parched lips. 'Why should you think that?'

'Why indeed,' he conceded, with a certain air of resignation. 'Do you mind if I sit down? I'm beat.'

Fliss blew out a breath. 'I—why, no. Please.' She gestured towards the chairs but he flopped down on the sofa instead. 'Um—can I get you anything? A drink? A cup of tea or coffee? Or a sandwich? You can't have had much time to get anything to eat.'

'A Coke would be fine,' he said wearily, and she scurried into the kitchen to get one from the fridge. But her mind was still buzzing with why Graham might have gone to see him, and because she was sure it could be nothing good she wished he'd come straight to the point.

Morgan swallowed at least half the can of Coke in one gulp and then dropped the can on the table and sank back, his head resting on the flowered upholstery. 'That's better,' he said gratefully. 'I should have had a drink before I left. But after Bland departed I was too impatient to hang about and I just got back in the car and came on here.'

Fliss nodded, but she could feel her apprehension expanding with every word he said. She couldn't imagine why Graham had felt the need to confide in Morgan, unless he'd given him a distorted view of today's events.

That seemed only too likely, and before Morgan could accuse her of anything she said the first thing that came into her head. 'He—Graham, that is—told me you're renting an apartment in Salisbury,' she said, trying not to sound resentful. 'When you said you were leaving London, I never imagined you meant you were moving into this area.'

Morgan's mouth compressed. 'You don't like it?'

'Like what?'

'What you just said: me moving into this area?'

'Oh.' Fliss was nonplussed. 'Well, it's nothing to do with me, is it?'

'It's everything to do with you,' retorted Morgan harshly. 'And I think we're getting away from the point.'

'Oh, yes, the point,' murmured Fliss uneasily, moving round her chair and perching on the arm. 'So—what has Graham been saying about me? Whatever it is, I don't think you should put too much faith in his beliefs.'

Morgan pushed himself forward in his seat, a frown creasing his brow now. 'You're saying he might have some reason for lying to me, is that it? My God, what could he hope to gain from that?'

'Who knows?' But Fliss's lips were tight. 'Why don't you tell me what he said and we might find out?'

CHAPTER FOURTEEN

MORGAN breathed deeply, and then, pressing his hands down on the cushions at either side of him, he got to his feet. It was obvious that what she'd said had given him pause, and she watched somewhat anxiously as he paced across to the hearth.

When he took off his overcoat and flung it down on the chair next to hers, Fliss stiffened automatically, and he gave her a piercing look before moving away. 'I believe he told you that Linda had been to see me,' he declared abruptly, and Fliss's eyes widened as the ramifications of that statement sank in.

'Linda?' she exclaimed. 'Linda—Giles?'

'I don't believe I know any other Lindas,' he retorted brusquely. 'Bland said you'd assumed I was living with another woman.'

'*I'd* assumed?' Fliss swallowed back the urge to tell Morgan that it was Graham who had made that assumption. This wasn't the moment to defend herself about that. 'She's not staying with you?' she asked instead, trying to sound casual, but the oath Morgan uttered was anything but off-hand.

'Of course she's not staying with me,' he snarled, rounding on her angrily. 'What do you think I am? Unlike Bland, I wouldn't get involved with another man's wife. Oh—' He held up his hand. 'I know he thought I was dead; you don't have to tell me. But I've never been interested in Linda Giles. For God's sake you know that!'

Fliss expelled a breath. Of course, he was right. And had she known it was Linda Giles at Morgan's door she might not have been so willing to jump to the wrong conclusion.

But when Graham had mentioned the other woman she'd immediately thought the worst.

'So—what was she doing in Salisbury?' she asked, not yet prepared to take all the blame, and he sighed.

'She knew we weren't together, so she thought I might be—lonely,' he told her flatly. 'She made some excuse about wanting to see where I was living, and like a fool I let her in.'

Fliss took a steadying breath. 'But—nothing happened?'

'Are you kidding?' Morgan gave her a bitter look. 'If I'd wanted to sleep with Linda Giles, I could have done so years ago. No, as soon as she started coming on to me, I threw her out.'

Fliss nodded. 'Well, he—Graham, that is—didn't know who she was, of course.'

'And you put two and two together and made six?'

'Something like that.' Fliss picked up one of the exercise books she had been marking, and smoothed its cover. 'What was I supposed to think? It—it was obvious you didn't want me—'

'What?'

His exclamation was so vehement, Fliss pressed the exercise book to her chest, and drew back in some alarm. But she knew she had to finish what she'd started. 'It's true,' she said defensively. Then she blushed. 'You were so—cruel to me the—the last time you were here.'

Morgan halted in front of her. 'I was cruel to you?' he echoed disbelievingly. 'Give me a break!'

'You were.' Fliss couldn't look at him so she looked at the exercise book instead. 'When you walked out of here that evening, I was sure you'd never want to speak to me again.'

Morgan swore again, and just when she thought he was going to walk away once more he bent and hauled her bodily to her feet. 'I was angry,' he said harshly. 'I felt—

humiliated. I was sure you'd only taken pity on me to ease your conscience.'

The book dropped to the floor as Fliss stared at him. 'But you must have known—' she began, but he cut her off.

'What must I have known?' Morgan's eyes were dark with anguish. 'As far as I was concerned, you didn't want me, you wanted another man.'

'But you can't have thought—'

'That you were using me as a substitute?' Morgan grimaced. 'When you're feeling as low as I am, you'll believe anything. Trust me.'

Fliss couldn't believe it. 'But you were so—so—'

'What?' His hands massaged her shoulders. 'Tell me!'

'Well—' She caught her lip between her teeth. 'You seemed to hate me, somehow.'

'I did,' he muttered roughly, his hands sliding across her shoulders to her neck and cupping it between his palms. 'How was I supposed to feel? You'd given me a taste of heaven and I wanted more.'

Fliss blinked. 'You're not serious,' she cried, not daring to believe what she thought she was hearing, and his hand at her nape pulled her against his chest.

'Of course I'm serious,' he affirmed, his thumb finding the sensitive hollow behind her ear. His lips parted. 'You know, I can feel your pulse and it's racing. Does this mean that what Bland hinted at is true?'

Fliss, whose hand had been halfway to his face, now spread her palm against the fine wool of his jacket. 'I—I suppose that depends on what he told you,' she murmured as apprehension reared its ugly head again.

'Well—' Morgan was thoughtful '—he said he believed that you and he were—how did he put it?—Ah, yes: incompatible. That was the term he used.' His thumb stroked her cheek. 'He wanted me to know that even if you and I got a divorce the fact that you two wouldn't be getting engaged again was a mutual decision.'

Fliss caught her breath. She knew she should be angry at Graham for pretending that their parting had been a civilised affair, but right now such an emotion was beyond her. She was so relieved that he'd accepted the situation as it was, and if he'd attempted to save his face—and salve his conscience—by trying to bring her and Morgan together she was prepared to overlook the rest.

'Th—that's what he said,' she got out now, her eyes drawn irresistibly to Morgan's mouth. 'Well, yes. We have—decided we're not suited, after all.' She dug a finger into his lapel. 'I—I wasn't sure you'd care any more.'

'Oh, I care,' said Morgan thickly, his lips hovering a few centimetres above her mouth. 'Too much, I used to think when I was stuck at Jamara. Did you know I kept a snapshot of you all the time I was imprisoned? As luck would have it, I'd been studying it on my way to the airport, and I shoved it in the pocket of my jeans when they stopped the car.' He grimaced. 'I was lucky, I guess. They threw my watch and wallet into the inferno. But it was months before I could look at your picture again without it tearing me apart.'

'Oh, Morgan—'

'So you've no need to doubt my feelings. The point is, do you still care about me?'

'How can you doubt it?' Fliss expelled an unsteady breath. 'After—after what happened, do you have to ask me that?'

'Oh, yes.' Morgan was resolute. 'I want there to be no more misunderstandings between us. If you stay with me now, it's for ever. I'm not like Bland. I'm not big enough to give you up.'

'Oh, Morgan…' Her voice broke on the word, and she felt the tears spilling down her cheeks. 'You're not like Graham,' she whispered, slipping her arms about his neck. One day she'd tell him how she knew that, but not today.

'I—I told him I loved you. I do. I don't think I ever stopped loving you. I realised that afternoon when I—when we—'

'Made love,' Morgan finished huskily, and then bent his head and covered her mouth with his.

It was midnight when Fliss tiptoed down the stairs to get a drink of water. Morgan was still sound asleep, and she'd spent several poignant minutes watching him before sliding off the bed. He looked so much younger with all the lines of stress smoothed away. For the first time she let herself believe what was happening. Morgan was back, he still loved her, and they were together.

It was chilly in the kitchen, but she hardly felt it. There was a warming feeling of contentment in her belly, and the fire that Morgan had ignited in her heart. She loved him, she thought giddily. How had she ever doubted it? Had she been so afraid of being hurt again?

Deciding a cup of tea might be more acceptable, she filled the kettle, wrapping her arms about herself as she waited for it to boil. All she was wearing was Morgan's old shirt which she'd put on without thinking, and its hem barely skimmed the tops of her thighs.

Her breasts felt hypersensitive against the cloth, but that was hardly surprising, she thought, closing her eyes as images of Morgan's lovemaking filled her head. Even the memory of his touch brought her body to full awareness, and she couldn't wait to go back upstairs and assure herself he was really there.

His arms closing around her from behind was Fliss's first indication that Morgan wasn't upstairs any longer. He drew her back against him and she realised at once that he was fully aroused. 'I missed you,' he said, his hands sliding possessively over her stomach. One hand dipped between her legs. 'Mmm, I see you were missing me, too.'

Fliss shivered. 'Morgan,' she choked, her breath catching in her throat at her own instantaneous response to his caress. 'You'll get cold,' she protested, when she could breathe again, and realised that he was naked as well. 'Morgan—God, don't do that. I want to make some tea.'

'Oh, well, if you'd rather,' he said mockingly, letting her go, and she gave him a wary look. 'It's okay,' he added, when he realised she was anxious. 'I can wait.' His eyes darkened. 'I'll go and keep the bed warm, shall I? Just don't take too long.'

Fliss swallowed, overwhelmingly tempted to follow him out of the door. 'Do you want any tea—or a sandwich?' she called after him.

And his, 'You know what I want,' drifted provocatively down the stairs.

Fliss and Morgan flew out to Nyanda to attend the millennium celebrations. Fliss was eight months pregnant at the time, and Morgan had been doubtful about her travelling so far. But as they were travelling in the president's plane, with the president's own doctor in attendance, Fliss had assured him she'd be perfectly all right. Besides, she wanted to be there when Morgan was presented with his award, and she was eager to meet the man who'd played such a significant role in her life.

Nevertheless, it was quite an ordeal, arriving in Nyanda at the end of one of the hottest months of the year. Fliss found it especially trying as they'd had snow in England at Christmas. She and Morgan had spent the holiday with Morgan's parents at Tudor Cross, and his mother had been most anxious that nothing untoward should threaten the life of their first grandchild.

Still, their rooms in the president's palace were very comfortable. The building was situated in the hills just outside Kantanga, and although there was no air conditioning in the palace its walls were thick, which muted the heat, and the breezes that blew up from the ocean were very welcome. In addition to which, all the walls and floors were marble, and Fliss pottered about quite happily in her bare feet.

There was to be a government reception on the eve of the millennium. A cocktail party was due to start at six o'clock, and President Mdola and his guests would dine at eight. Then, afterwards, he would present various awards for bravery, with a firework display commencing precisely on the stroke of midnight.

Morgan was concerned that such an exhausting evening would be too much for Fliss. Although they'd been in Nyanda for three days already, he wasn't sure she was strong enough to stand the heat.

'I'll be fine,' she assured him, from her position on the bed, watching him as he got ready. 'Julius—' she hadn't quite got used to calling the president by his given name yet '—Julius says I can sit down during all the ceremonial displays, and this gown he's given me is ideal for this climate.'

'Mmm.' Morgan gave up trying to fasten his tie and came to lean across her so that she could do it for him. 'Well, I must say it's attractive,' he conceded, running a possessive hand over the mound of her belly. His lips twitched as he felt the baby move against his palm. 'So long as you remember you're my woman, not his.'

'Your woman!' Fliss's eyes danced. 'I think you're adapting to Nyandan customs far too well.'

'Never that,' he said huskily, coming down on the bed beside her. 'This place will always remind me of what I nearly lost.'

'Well, you didn't lose anything, did you?' she told him softly. 'And who knows? Maybe those four years taught us to value what we have. Tomorrow's a new millennium, and we're together. That's what's important. Us, and our baby.' She covered his hand. 'Did you feel that? I think he agrees with us.'

* * *

Fliss started to feel uncomfortable during the cocktail party. At first, she put it down to standing for so long, and she sought one of the satin couches that were set against the wall. She felt much better once she was off her feet, and she breathed a sigh of relief. The last thing she wanted to do was cause a scene.

'Are you too hot, Felicity?'

To her embarrassment, President Mdola was standing over her, but when she would have got to her feet he waved her back. 'Relax, please,' he said pleasantly, joining her on the couch. 'I'm happy to see you liked the gift I sent you.'

Fliss flushed, and looked down at the flowing sari-like garment she was wearing. It was made of a delicious shade of turquoise silk, and was ideal for these conditions. 'I love it,' she said simply. 'It was very kind of you to give it to me. It's a much cooler material than any of the gowns I've brought from home.'

'It was my pleasure,' said Julius Mdola firmly, sipping his cocktail. 'And I'd like to tell you that I much appreciate you and Morgan coming here tonight. This is a special time for me; a special time for all of us. Which we may not have been able to celebrate without your husband's help.'

Fliss bent her head. 'No.'

Julius frowned. 'I suspect you haven't forgiven me for allowing you to think he hadn't survived the ambush,' he murmured softly, and Fliss wondered if her face had given her away. 'I'd like to tell you why I kept that information from you,' he continued. 'I want you to know it wasn't just for my sake.'

Fliss frowned. 'Please, it doesn't matter...'

'It does.' Julius gently touched her hand. 'I don't even know if you'll believe what I have to tell you. You had to know our—late—president to understand.'

'Oh, really—'

'If General Ungave had known that your husband had survived the ambush, his life would have been in real danger,' he persisted. 'After all, he'd have known exactly why we needed your husband's help. That was why my men had orders to destroy Morgan's belongings. Ungave's enemies—and some of his friends—seldom escaped his vengeance. One way or another, he'd have made sure that Morgan didn't survive.'

Fliss gasped. 'I can't believe it.'

'No. Well, as no doubt Morgan's told you, it wasn't a pretty war. No wars are pretty, of course, but some are more honourable than others. I regret General Ungave was not an honourable man.'

Fliss shook her head. 'Did Morgan know this?'

'No.' Julius sighed. 'I fear that, given the choice between his life and your peace of mind, he would have chosen the honourable option. I could not risk that. Morgan had become my friend. In my religion, a friend is worth his weight in gold.'

Fliss allowed her breath to escape in a sudden rush. Morgan must know this now, but he had never said a word to her. She guessed he had been protecting her: defending her right to have found someone else.

She'd learned so much about her husband during the past nine months. The capacity he had for forgiveness; his capacity for loving her. When she'd told him about Graham, he'd been angry, of course, but he'd deferred to her wish not to resurrect what was done. Whether he'd have been so generous if Graham had remained in Whittersley was another matter. But in the event Reverend Bland had found another living at the opposite end of the country.

Meanwhile, Fliss and Morgan had bought a house in Salisbury. It meant they were near to Fliss's aunt Sophie, and Fliss could go on working at the school. She'd left now, of course, because of the baby, but the option was there to return to teaching if she wished.

Fliss was about to tell Julius how grateful she was that he'd confided in her when a pain like a knife caused her to catch her breath. Oh, God, she thought anxiously, surely she couldn't be having the baby. It was three more weeks at least until it was due.

'Is something wrong?'

Ever alert to any eventuality, Julius was staring at her now with concerned eyes. But the pain had subsided again, and Fliss assured herself it had just been indigestion. She'd had a peach before leaving for the reception. It had been deliciously ripe, but perhaps it hadn't been the most sensible thing to eat.

'I'm fine,' she said now, but she couldn't help glancing about the room for her husband. He was standing with a group of the president's army officers, and she guessed they were reminiscing about the war. 'It's been a long day,' she added, unable to resist laying a hand on her stomach. There was no movement now, and she realised there hadn't been for some time.

'So many people wanted to attend the reception,' said Julius. 'And I'm afraid the humidity is rather high. We'll be having dinner soon and the fans in the banqueting hall are more efficient. But I must thank you once again for coming to Nyanda at such an—' he hesitated '—such an—exhausting time.'

'We both wanted to come.' Fliss couldn't let him think otherwise. 'And I'm sorry if I was—offhand when we were introduced.'

'I think you're a beautiful woman,' said Julius loyally, 'and my friend is very fortunate. I understand now why he found it so hard to talk about you. He was tortured by the knowledge that you might find someone else.'

Fliss was moved by his sincerity, staring at her husband with the love she felt for him shining in her eyes. But then, once again, the pain drove through her and left her so breathless, she couldn't hide her discomfort from Julius.

'Felicity!' he was exclaiming, raising his hand to summon one of the stewards, when Morgan came striding across the floor.

'What is it, Fliss?' he demanded, grasping her hands and squatting down beside her. 'Do you feel faint? Would you like me to take you back to our suite?'

'I think—I think—'

Fliss couldn't get the words out as once again a contraction gripped her abdomen, and Julius gently touched the other man's sleeve. 'I have some experience in these matters,' he said softly, 'and I believe your wife has started to have your baby, Morgan. Stay with her while I organise my guests.'

Morgan took Julius's place on the couch as the other man had his stewards announce that dinner was ready. Whether it was or not, his efficient staff had soon emptied the reception room. There were a few interested glances in their direction, but most of the guests were too polite to stare, and when the doors had closed behind them Julius hurried back to his friends.

'Come,' he said. 'I've made arrangements for Felicity to be examined by my own doctor. We have a medical facility here at the palace, and I'm sure she will be quite comfortable there.'

'But—the baby—' said Fliss weakly, and Julius gave her a reassuring smile.

'Will have dual citizenship,' he said. 'Which is just as it should be, don't you think?'

Fliss and Morgan's son was born as the dawn was breaking. It had been a long night for both of them, but although Fliss was exhausted the sight of her son's small face drove all thoughts of sleeping out of her head.

'Oh, Morgan,' she breathed, when he handed the baby to her. 'He's just like you. His hair is almost white.'

'Just like me,' agreed Morgan, with a wry smile, seating himself on the bed beside her. He cupped her face in his hands. 'Oh, Fliss, thank God that you're all right. I've spent most of the night berating myself for bringing you here. I shouldn't have been so selfish. You weren't really fit to travel so far.'

'I wouldn't have let you go without me,' declared Fliss staunchly. 'The last time I did that, you were away for four whole years.' She covered his hand with one of hers. 'I love you.'

'And I love you,' he muttered. 'More than you'll ever know.'

'Oh, I have a fairly good idea,' murmured Fliss softly, returning her attention to their baby. 'Look, darling, his eyes are open. He obviously thinks this isn't such a bad place, after all.'

'Right now, it's as close as I'll get to heaven,' muttered Morgan roughly. 'I can't think of anywhere else I'd rather be. I said as much to Dr Obote before he went to inform Julius that we had a son, and I'm pretty sure that he agreed with me.'

Fliss smiled, and then she caught her lip between her teeth. 'Oh, Morgan,' she cried. 'You missed the presentation. You should have left me here and enjoyed the celebrations.'

'As if.' Morgan was sardonic. 'My darling, I was present at the only presentation I care about.' He bent his head and rubbed his lips against hers. 'What better celebration of the new millennium could we have than this?'

**Race to the altar—
Maxie, Darcy and Polly are**

The **HUSBAND** *Hunters*

in a fabulous new
Harlequin Presents® miniseries by

LYNNE GRAHAM

These three women have each been left a share of
their late godmother's estate—but only if they marry
withing a year and remain married for six months....

Maxie's story: **Married to a Mistress**
Harlequin Presents #2001, January 1999

Darcy's story: **The Vengeful Husband**
Harlequin Presents #2007, February 1999

Polly's story: **Contract Baby**
Harlequin Presents #2013, March 1999

Will they get to the altar in time?

Available in January, February and March 1999
wherever Harlequin books are sold.

HARLEQUIN®
Makes any time special ™

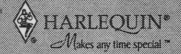

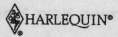

Not The Same Old Story!

 Exciting, glamorous romance stories that take readers around the world.

 Sparkling, fresh and tender love stories that bring you pure romance.

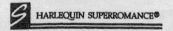 Bold and adventurous—Temptation is strong women, bad boys, great sex!

 Provocative and realistic stories that celebrate life and love.

 Contemporary fairy tales—where anything is possible and where dreams come true.

HARLEQUIN®
INTRIGUE® Heart-stopping, suspenseful adventures that combine the best of romance and mystery.

LOVE & LAUGHTER™ Humorous and romantic stories that capture the lighter side of love.

Coming Next Month

HARLEQUIN PRESENTS®

THE BEST HAS JUST GOTTEN BETTER!

#2001 MARRIED TO A MISTRESS Lynne Graham
(The Husband Hunters)
If Maxie Kendall marries within a year, she'll inherit a fortune.
As she must clear her father's debts, she needs to find a
husband—*fast!* Greek tycoon Angelos Petronides definitely
wants to bed her...but will he want to wed her?

#2002 ONE NIGHT IN HIS ARMS Penny Jordan
Sylvie had been determined to act cool and distant for this
meeting with Ranulf Carrington—after all his cruel words last
time. But her body still ached for his...and Sylvie knew she'd
do almost anything for just one night in his arms....

#2003 THE SEDUCTION PROJECT Miranda Lee
(Presents Passion)
Molly's makeover hadn't succeeded in getting Liam Delaney
interested in her. It was time for an ultimatum. If Liam didn't
want her to lose her virginity to another admirer, he'd just
have to make love to her himself!

#2004 THE BABY SECRET Helen Brooks
(Expecting!)
Victoria's marriage had only lasted one night! It seemed
her husband, Zac, had a mistress—so Victoria had fled
immediately. But Zac had found her...and wasn't keen to
give her up. And he didn't even know about the baby yet....

#2005 THE PLAYBOY AND THE NANNY Anne McAllister
When a wealthy businessman offered Mari a job as a live-in
nanny, she wasn't expecting her charge to be a rebellious
thirty-two-year-old playboy! But Nikos Costanides didn't
want to be reformed...he wanted to seduce Mari!

#2006 A SUITABLE MISTRESS Cathy Williams
Dane Sutherland was rich, powerful and sinfully gorgeous. He
had it all—but he wanted more! He wanted Suzanne...and she
was equally determined not to fall into his arms...or his bed!